"Don't you fee

nothing touches you. Nothing bothers you. You're always in control."

He freed his fingers from hers, reversed his grip and held her palm to the side of his neck.

"Don't mistake control for a lack of feeling, Chantal. I feel everything," he said. "I'm as worried as you are about the welfare of the hostages, maybe more, because I've seen what can happen when situations like this go wrong." He pressed her hand more firmly to his skin. "I'm concentrating on my duty so I can shut everything else out, but I can't turn it off entirely."

She shuddered. "That's what I mean. I can't turn it off, either."

"And if things weren't already complicated enough, for the last ten minutes, I've felt your body under mine and your hair tickling my cheek. A minute ago I felt the curve of your breast under your jacket and right now I can feel the trembling in your fingers. I've been doing my damnedest to ignore all of that, too."

Leave it to Mitch not to beat around the bush.

Dear Reader,

Army of Two was a labor of love for me right from the start. I've had a crush on Major Mitch Redinger since he popped up in the first book of my original EAGLE SQUADRON series. He was so noble, so dedicated to his men and his missions—and so handsome in his uniform!—he deserved a story of his own. Many of you readers agreed.

The only problem was, I had given him a wedding ring. Luckily, I hadn't given him a wife to go with it. Believe me, I combed back through the books to make sure she was no longer in the picture. Those stories had been my first experience with a miniseries, and I hadn't realized when I started how many details had to be kept straight. I can only hope that no one was too confused by one character's changing eye color. Maybe he'd decided to wear colored contacts and had forgotten to tell me.

Anyway, I knew Mitch wouldn't give his love easily a second time. Thus I needed to find a character like Chantal, who had loved him first. To my delight, her crush on the major turned out to be even bigger than mine.

Happy reading,

Ingrid

INGRID WEAVER

Army of Two

ROMANTIC
SUSPENSE

Recycling programs for this product may not exist in your area.

ISBN-13: 978-0-373-27691-2

ARMY OF TWO

This edition published by arrangement with Harlequin Books S.A.

For questions and comments about the quality of this book please contact us at Customer_eCare@Harlequin.ca.

Visit Silhouette Books at www.eHarlequin.com

Printed in U.S.A.

Books by Ingrid Weaver

Silhouette Romantic Suspense

True Blue #570
True Lies #660
On the Way to a Wedding… #761
Engaging Sam #875
What the Baby Knew #939
Cinderella's Secret Agent #1076
Fugitive Hearts #1101
Under the King's Command #1184
**Eye of the Beholder* #1204
**Seven Days to Forever* #1216
**Aim for the Heart* #1258
In Destiny's Shadow #1329
†*The Angel and the Outlaw* #1352
†*Loving the Lone Wolf* #1369
†*Romancing the Renegade* #1389
***Her Baby's Bodyguard* #1604
***Accidental Commando* #1614
***Army of Two* #1621

*Eagle Squadron
†Payback
**Eagle Squadron: Countdown

Silhouette Special Edition

The Wolf and the Woman's Touch #1056

Silhouette Books

Family Secrets
"The Insider"

INGRID WEAVER

propped an old manual typewriter on her children's playroom table to write her first novel. Twenty-six books later there's a computer in place of the typewriter and a RITA® Award on the corner of her grown-up-sized desk, but the joy she found in creating her first story hasn't changed. "I write because life is full of possibilities," Ingrid says, "and the best ones are those that we make." Ingrid lives on a farm in southern Ontario, where she gardens in the summer and knits in the winter. You can visit Ingrid's Web site at www.ingridweaver.com.

This book is dedicated to the real heroes, the men and women who serve in our armed forces.

Chapter 1

The Aerie perched on an outcropping of rock that thrust straight out from the hillside. Its entire front wall was made of glass, providing a bird's-eye vantage point that wasn't for the faint of heart. From the second-floor gallery, Chantal Leduc could see across the lake to the line of distant mountains that held the northern end of the Appalachian Trail. Above it all stretched a wild and endless expanse of sky that never failed to lift her spirits.

The view was only one of the reasons she loved this place. She loved the homey smell of wood smoke that lingered in the log walls, and the solid, here-to-stay sound her footsteps made on the plank floors. There were misty mornings when the lake was a mirror and the air was so pure it tasted sweet. On clear nights, the stars were as thick as the pebbles on the shore. Every winding trail strewn with orange pine needles and each majestic spruce that swept its branches up the hillside had a regal, timeless beauty. Here was the peace she'd struggled to achieve. Here was sanctuary.

None of that would change simply because *he* was coming. He would only stay a week. She could manage that.

"Miss Leduc?"

Chantal curled her hands around the gallery railing and peered into the lobby. The boy who looked up at her was all pre-adolescent arms and legs, as eager to please as a puppy. His father was the cook, his mother the resort's accountant and assistant manager. The pair had been part of the package when Chantal had taken over the business, although they felt more like family than employees. She remembered how Henry had been a mere toddler the first summer she'd come to work here. Some of the furniture in the dining room still bore the scratches of his toy trucks. "Yes, Henry?"

"I think that's them," he said, pointing out the window.

She scanned the sky, and her hands tightened on the railing. He'd picked out what she hadn't yet seen. There was a speck to the southeast above the horizon that glinted in the rays of the lowering sun. Though it was too far to distinguish any details, it had to be the helicopter they were expecting. No one strayed this far into Maine's North Woods by accident. "Let your dad know we'll be serving dinner in an hour," she said.

He waved and disappeared beneath the gallery. Chantal could hear the rhythmic thump of the aircraft now, vibrating through the walls and windows. She remained where she was and watched the speck grow larger while she went through a mental checklist. Linens. Towels. Food and liquor. Wood for the fireplaces. Gas for the outboards.

The storage batteries from the solar panels were fully charged and should handle their power needs, but there was also plenty of extra fuel for the emergency generator. "Rustic luxury" was how she described the atmosphere in her brochures, and that's what she aimed to deliver. The Petherick Corporation had paid handsomely for the exclusive use of the lodge for a full seven days.

The request hadn't been unusual. The Aerie's isolation made it an ideal site for corporate retreats. Chantal wasn't the only one who had discovered the restorative powers of this place. She had a growing client base of city-weary executives. Normally she enjoyed providing the means for them to unwind, do team building or entertain their customers. This was what she did, and she was good at it. She should be feeling a pleasant glow of anticipation right about now.

Yet what she felt was too intense to be called pleasant. Major Mitchell Redinger would be on that helicopter. And the knowledge made her feel like an inept teenager, as awkward and eager to please as Henry.

On the inside, anyway. Outwardly, it had to be business as usual. So what if Mitch was on his way here? It shouldn't make any difference. He was part of the delegation from the army that the Petherick Corporation was trying to woo. He would eat the food she had chosen, sleep in one of the bedrooms she had decorated, watch the same sunrise that she did and perhaps stroll the same pine-needled paths. Just like any other guest.

Yes, and that's how she had to treat him. Like any other guest. It had been seventeen years, after all. He might not even remember the last time they'd seen each other.

But she did. Oh, God, how could she forget a humiliation like that? Every excruciating moment of it had been burned into her memory.

"Miss Leduc, did you lock the door to the meeting room? I can't get it open."

Chantal drew in a steadying breath, straightened her spine and turned away from the railing. One of the college students who had hired on for the season was balancing a tray of water glasses in one hand while she used the other to shove against the door at the far end of the gallery. She should have realized at the Aerie, only the guest rooms needed locks.

Chantal eyed the wavering glasses as she hurried forward. "Hang on, Rhonda," she said. She grasped the knob in both hands and gave it a sharp, upward jerk. The latch clicked immediately. "The wood swells sometimes," she said. "Especially when we get the kind of downpours we had last week. It's one of the lodge's idiosyncrasies."

Rhonda thanked her and carried the glasses inside. She was followed by her brother, Tommy, another student, who was carrying a large bottle of purified water on his shoulder. He installed it on the cooler opposite the long slab of polished pink granite that served as the top of the conference table. The room faced the hillside rather than the lake. Only yards from the window, a living wall of evergreens blended with maples that had been colored by frost.

The room Chantal had prepared for Mitch was at the front, with a view of the water. She'd thought he would enjoy that. And for her own peace of mind, the selection put him as far as possible from her own suite at the back of the staff quarters. Cowardly, perhaps. Unnecessary, for sure. He was no more likely to care whether he saw her now than he had cared seventeen years ago.

She gave the meeting room a quick scan to ensure there were sufficient chairs, though there would be only nine in the party, then headed for the back staircase and went to check on the progress in the kitchen. By the time she walked into the lobby, the helicopter was practically level with the front windows. The black-and-gold logo of the Petherick Corporation flashed from its gleaming-white fuselage as it did a hovering turn to line up for its landing. She pressed her palm to her stomach, annoyed to feel butterflies.

That was how Mitch always used to affect her. He'd been tall, dark and as dashing as any young girl could dream. A romantic hero who had come to life in an army uniform. In her eyes he'd been perfect.

Of course, the reality had been something else entirely, she thought, pulling on her jacket as she stepped outside. No man could have lived up to the expectations she'd put on him. In her head, she knew that. She understood it wasn't fair to resent Mitch simply because he hadn't shared her fantasy.

But he'd been her first love...and the first man to break her heart. No woman ever forgot that. How on earth was she supposed to pretend indifference?

"I learned about this place from my cousin." Graham Petherick leaned closer to Mitch and shouted into his headset over the noise of the engine. "He spent two weeks here this past June, said the togue practically jumped into his boat. That's what the locals call lake trout."

Mitch craned his neck to look out the window. There was a wooden dock and what appeared to be a boathouse at the lakeshore. A long, switchbacking staircase rose from the water's edge to a large building constructed mainly of logs and glass. Like the staircase, the structure appeared to cling to the bare rock. An observation deck jutted from one side while a mix of maples and pine cloaked the hill on the other where the slope was less steep. Although, to call it a hill didn't do it justice. Before it had been worn down by glaciers and a few millennia of weather, it would have been a mountain. "I didn't know you were a fisherman," he said.

Graham laughed. "I'm not. Never saw the appeal of trying to outwit a fish. I'll take a rifle over a fishing rod any day."

That figured, Mitch thought. Graham had made his first million more than four decades ago manufacturing firearms. He was currently building another fortune by producing far more powerful—and more expensive—firepower for the U.S. Military. He was a good businessman and never failed to deliver high-quality products. Much of the Petherick Corporation's success was due to its policy of understanding what the customer needed ahead of time.

That was the purpose of this week in the North Woods with the company's top executives. It wasn't about sales, it was about determining the next direction the development department should take. From what Mitch had understood, they were looking into a new signal-dampening device that could neutralize an enemy's detection systems. Graham had invited Mitch and three other army officers because he'd expected to pick their collective brains, not their wallets. Not at this stage, anyway.

The helicopter drifted over the roof of the lodge and headed toward a cleared area on the crest of the hill above where a white circle had been painted on the rock. Moments later, the landing gear bumped against the ground. Graham buttoned a red-and-black plaid jacket over his paunch, slapped Mitch on the shoulder and moved toward the exit door. "Grab your gear, ladies and gentlemen," he shouted. "My pilot wants to get back by nightfall, so once this bird leaves, we're on our own."

The men and women from Petherick Corporation who

had accompanied Graham didn't appear as enthusiastic about their destination as their boss did. They consisted of two vice presidents, the company comptroller and the director of research, and they looked as if they'd come straight from the office. The backwash from the prop blades tore at their suits as they ducked their heads and dragged their wheeled suitcases across the rocky hilltop.

The army men were dressed in more casual clothes. From what Mitch had heard, the general and both of the colonels who'd been invited on this trip often consulted with the Petherick Corporation. They spent most of their time riding desks at the Pentagon. He'd hate being saddled with a duty like that—he far preferred to be in the field with his men. Since this was Mitch's first time at one of Graham's brainstorming sessions, he hadn't met these officers before today. He wasn't familiar with anyone here except Graham.

And Chantal Leduc.

It had been almost two decades since he'd seen her. He'd been surprised to learn she'd ended up at a resort in Maine, of all places. That was a puzzle. He couldn't picture the pampered child of his former commanding officer wanting to live in a setting this uncivilized.

The whine of the rotors increased, sending grit and dead leaves rippling across the rock. The helicopter lifted off more quickly than it had landed, did a quarter turn and dipped its nose toward the water as it headed back across the lake. Before the noise of its departure could fade, a slender woman had emerged from the woods at the crest of the hill and walked toward them.

She moved with the easy grace of a dancer, as if she heard music that no one else could. Black denim clung to her long legs and the curve of her hips. A suede jacket the color of chocolate hugged her shoulders while the evening breeze sent the ends of her long, dark hair teasing around her face. Her smile, her body language, everything about her projected control, confidence and poise.

This couldn't possibly be Chantal.

"Welcome to the Aerie," she said, offering her hand to Graham, who was in the lead of the group. "I'm Chantal Leduc."

Mitch tried not to stare. It was her, all right. Her voice still had the distinctive, smokey undertone that he would recognize anywhere. Instead of the bubbly enthusiasm that used to infuse her words, she now spoke with unhurried, perfect enunciation, just as her mother had. Once again, he was struck by how odd it was to find her here. Chantal had adored her mother and had been on her way to becoming a carbon copy of her, but that woman would have been more comfortable on the veranda of a plantation house, ordering the servants to bring her more mint juleps. She wouldn't have been caught dead presiding over a resort in the wilderness.

A loon warbled its howling cry from somewhere on the lake. Several people in the group startled and looked around nervously. Chantal calmed them with a smile and paused to explain what they'd heard.

A boy and a couple who appeared to be in their early twenties arrived to help carry the guests' luggage. Only Petherick's suit-clad people accepted the offer. Chantal politely directed everyone toward a graveled path bordered with rounded stones that led downward through the trees. Mitch slung the strap of his duffel bag on his shoulder. Although she had smiled vaguely in his direction, she hadn't yet met his gaze.

She had to have known he was coming. Was she trying to postpone the awkward moment, or did she intend to ignore him for the entire week? She'd had a penchant for disregarding reality when she'd been a teenager. He wondered whether that hadn't changed. He stepped forward before she could follow the others. "Hello, Chantal."

To her credit, there was no hesitation in her response. "Good evening, Major Redinger." She didn't offer her hand. Instead, she gave him the same, gracious smile that she'd given when she'd talked about the loon. "It's nice to see you again."

"It's been a long time."

"It has indeed, Major."

Major, not Mitch. She was drawing a distinct line. He wasn't sure why that irritated him. He should be pleased. "How is the general?" he asked. "I haven't seen him since he retired."

"My father's well, thank you."

"I heard he moved to Arizona."

"Yes. The drier climate seems to agree with him."

"That's good."

"Yes." She inclined her head toward the gap in the trees and started moving once more. "I hope you enjoy your stay at the Aerie. I'll show you to your room so you can unpack before dinner. Our cook is preparing grilled trout with blueberry sauce."

That was as personal as she would allow the conversation to get. Mitch fell into step beside her, studying her as they walked, trying to spot traces of the girl's face in the woman's. The pale blue eyes that had been her most outstanding feature had new shadows in their depths. There were dramatic hollows beneath her cheekbones and a lushness to her lips. He could see that the prettiness she'd possessed as a teenager had honed itself into a mature beauty.

It wasn't only her face that had matured, either. The

blouse she wore under her suede jacket pulled taut across a pair of generous breasts. He'd already noticed her attractively curved hips. Combined with the way she moved, her body projected a ripe sexuality. Little Chantal was now a woman in her prime.

And despite his best intentions, his body responded.

Damn. He hadn't expected this. He'd thought that almost two decades would have dulled the reaction.

Nevertheless, the image of how Chantal had looked when they'd parted flitted through Mitch's mind. He strove to block it out, as he always did.

He didn't want to remember. She belonged to a chapter of his past that he preferred to forget.

The air was thick with the smell of fuel, sweat and damp cement, but the hangar doors would remain closed until the men completed the loading. They couldn't run the risk of witnesses at this stage. Lewis Knox hadn't remained alive this long by being careless.

A thin, ponytailed figure moved through the illumination of the truck headlights and rounded the nose of the black chopper. It was Ted Bamford, their communications man. "I just got a message from our contact."

"Well?"

"They arrived four hours ago, right on schedule."

"Was Petherick with them?"

"Big as life."

"Any more details?"

"Like what?" Bamford snorted a laugh. "You're wondering how the fishing is?"

Lewis strove for patience. As long as he needed Bamford's skill with electronics, he had to put up with his attitude. "Names. Room assignments."

"Oh, right. I didn't get any names, but I did hear their rooms are on the top floor."

"What about the resort staff?"

"They're all tucked in for the night, behind the kitchen at the back."

Lewis unfolded the sketched floor plan their contact had provided and tilted it toward the light. So far, this was just as he'd expected. "All right. Once we block the rear exit, we'll bottle up the staff. The fewer we need to kill in the initial assault, the more hostages we'll have later. Which of the rooms were given to the military personnel?"

"I don't know. What difference does that make?"

"They're the only ones likely to offer resistance." He tapped his finger against each of the staircases. "We need to neutralize them before they can reach the exits. We'll strike before dawn. Hit hard and hit fast."

"I wouldn't worry about those army dudes. I thought your friend said Petherick only deals with desk jockeys. Guys who're already halfway out to pasture."

"Complacency can get you killed, Bamford."

He slapped one hand against the submachine gun that hung from his shoulder. "Not with what I'll be carrying."

Lewis refolded the sketch, stored it in his shirt pocket, then kicked Bamford's feet from under him and snatched the gun while he was on his way down. He pressed the end of the barrel against Bamford's throat to pin him on the floor. "Don't underestimate your adversary."

"What the hell… How'd you do that?"

"This is only one of the lessons the army taught me."

"Damn it, Knox. You're crazy."

He flicked down the safety and caressed the trigger.

"That's what they claimed. Maybe you'd like out. Is that what you want, Bamford? You want to quit?"

"I never said that."

"If you stay, you need to follow my orders."

"Sure. That's what I've been doing. Come on, man. Move the gun."

Lewis looked around him. The activity near the chopper had stopped. The flight crew were lounging against a fuel drum they should have been loading and were apparently indifferent to their comrade's fate. That wasn't the case with Taddeo, Brown and Dodson, three of the ten men who provided the muscle for the group. They watched eagerly, no doubt hoping for blood to be spilled.

This demonstration was for their sake as much as for Bamford's. When dealing with men like these, it was essential to establish who was in command. Like a pack of animals, they understood strength and little else. Lewis waited until he had made eye contact with every one of them, then lifted the gun barrel and used it to wave them back to work.

He had no illusions about the loyalty of the team he had assembled. They stuck with him for the sake of profit, not principles. Money was a good motivator.

But it wasn't as effective as fear.

Chapter 2

Chantal warmed her hands around her coffee mug as she walked along the floating dock. Streamers of mist rose from the lake, obscuring the line between water and air. The base of the staircase that zigzagged up the hillside was disappearing behind her, giving the illusion that the Aerie was floating on a cloud. The front windows reflected the lightening sky, though the sun wouldn't rise over the horizon for another half hour.

Petherick had kept his group in the meeting room until after midnight, so Chantal had assumed none of them would be getting up this early. She liked to take a few minutes for herself before she had to start the day. Yet she hadn't gone more than halfway to the end of the dock when the boards beneath her feet vibrated with the sounds of someone else's footsteps. She turned to look behind her.

A tall man in a black leather bomber-style jacket

materialized from the mist. She recognized him instinctively, even before he drew close enough for her to make out his features. Only one person had ever been able to give her pulse a bump like this.

Wonderful. So much for her few moments of peace. She took a sip of her coffee and put on her hostess smile. She could do this. The first night was already behind them. Only six more days and nights to go. "Good morning, Major. I see you found your way to the kitchen."

He was carrying a mug identical to hers. He lifted it in a salute as he reached her. "It looks as if we had the same idea. Hope you don't mind if I helped myself from that bowl of muffins on the sideboard, too."

"Not at all. I wasn't aware that anyone else was up. I'll put on some more coffee."

"Don't bother. The place was still quiet when I came outside. It seems we're the only early risers."

She should have remembered that about him. He used to go jogging before dawn whenever his schedule had allowed it. By the time his route had taken him past their house, his T-shirt would be damp and clinging to his chest, the muscles in his arms and legs gleaming. How many mornings had she waited by her window for the sound of his running shoes on the pavement? Those secret glimpses of his taut body used to fuel her imagination for the rest of the day.

She gulped another mouthful of coffee, then continued to move toward the end of the dock. "If you're interested in fishing, you're welcome to use any of our canoes while you're here."

"You have canoes? I didn't see any."

She gestured toward the boathouse behind them. "We've been storing them inside since a wandering moose put its hoof through the hull of one that had been left pulled up on the shore. They can be fitted with small outboard motors, but most of our guests prefer a quieter ride. We also have a traditional mahogany launch for touring."

He walked beside her, his arm almost—but not quite—touching hers. "Mahogany? It sounds like a classic."

"It is. We were lucky to obtain it."

"Sounds as if you do things old-school around here."

"We try to provide rustic luxury," she said, then grimaced inwardly at the trite response. She was sounding like one of her brochures.

The dock widened into a platform that held a group of Adirondack chairs. The wood was coated with dew, so neither of them sat. "How large is this lake?" he asked.

"The main body is around sixteen miles long and a mile wide. If you decide to explore any of the arms by canoe, you'd best take a map along. Or a guide."

"I'll endeavor not to get lost."

She realized belatedly how silly her caution must have sounded. "Many of our clients are city people," she said. "Of course, with your military training you wouldn't have any trouble finding your way."

"It's always wise to be familiar with the terrain before you set out. I took a look at the map in your lobby and saw that you have a network of hiking trails as well."

"Yes. Just let us know when you want to go and we'll arrange a packed lunch for you."

"Sounds good, but I'll have to wait and see what Graham has planned. It's his party."

"Any time you need anything, Major Redinger, just let me or one of my staff know."

He nodded and lifted his mug to his lips.

Chantal watched. She couldn't help herself. He had a beautifully shaped mouth. His upper lip was a sculpted bow, his lower one firmly masculine, and his smiles had packed quite a punch. That was one of the things that had first drawn her to him. The other officers who had served under her father had seemed to have only two expressions, stone or rock, but Mitch had been different. She'd seen humor in his steel-gray eyes and compassion in his face.

Yet he didn't look like a man who smiled often anymore. The lines on the sides of his mouth had deepened since she'd last seen him, giving his features a more chiseled appearance. The angle of his jaw appeared harder than it used to be. She wondered whether his skin still tasted the same.

"You might as well call me Mitch," he said. "There's no use pretending we're strangers."

"I'm not pretending anything," she said, although she knew it was a lie. There was no way she would let him know how his presence still had the power to affect her.

Why couldn't he have gained weight? Or lost his hair? Plenty of men got soft as they aged, yet Mitch only appeared harder. He would be forty-five by now, but in his leather jacket and his tan cargo pants, his body seemed as lean and fit as when he'd been twenty-eight. He had the slim hips and tight butt that were typical of a runner's build, and he would likely look the same at seventy. His dark brown hair was still thick. The touch of silver that she noticed at his temples only added to his attractiveness.

She glanced at the gold ring that gleamed on his left hand, then turned her gaze to the lake. There was nothing to see except the wall of mist, but it was preferable to looking at his wedding band.

He still wore it. That in itself was statement enough. She felt even more of a fool for the dreams about love that she'd once had. Her own marriage had been brutally short. She rarely thought about it these days. Obviously, the woman Mitch had chosen to give his heart to continued to hold it, even though she'd been dead for more than seven years.

"In a way, we *are* strangers, Mitch," she continued. "I'm not the same person I used to be. I doubt if you are, either."

"Time changes everyone."

"I heard you're based at Fort Bragg now."

"That's right."

"My father said you're commanding a Special Forces unit. Eagle Squadron, isn't it?"

"I'm surprised the topic came up. I wouldn't have thought you'd kept track."

She forced a laugh. Keep it light. Casual. "The general's the one who kept track. He likes to follow the careers of his officers. So don't worry. My stalking days are long over."

"You know what I meant, Chantal."

"Oh?"

"Going through these social niceties with me must be tough for you. We didn't part on the best of terms."

That had to be the understatement of the century. Leave it to Mitch to tackle the issue head-on. He'd had a penchant for directness when he'd been younger. She suspected his impatience with politics was one of the reasons why he hadn't risen above the rank of major. He was well suited to the independent, outside-the-box mind-set of the Special Forces.

She responded to his understatement with one of her own. "I suppose you could say our last encounter was somewhat awkward."

"As I recall, the final thing you told me was to go to hell."

"Now it's my turn to be surprised. I wouldn't have thought you'd remember that."

He shrugged, quiet apart from the subtle creak of his leather jacket.

"Kids tend to be dramatic," she said, wanting to fill the silence—and hating the fact that she did. She'd be damned if she was going to apologize.

"I hope my presence here won't be a problem for you."

She put on a smile that would have made her mother proud. And lied again. "Not at all. You're my guest, and it's my job to make your stay as pleasant as possible. Try to think of me as your host instead of a confused adolescent."

"I'll do my best."

Chantal swallowed the rest of what she wanted to say. Unfortunately, there was a lot because it had been simmering for a long time.

Yet as she'd just reminded him, in less than a week he'd be gone. As long as she kept her dealings with him on a professional basis, she could do this.

A fish splashed somewhere to their left. Mitch turned his head toward the sound as ripples bobbed across the water beneath the mist. "I wouldn't have expected to find you in a place like the Aerie, Chantal. Is this what you always wanted, to run a resort in Maine?"

No, I wanted to marry you, Mitch. I wanted you to ride in on your white charger and rescue me from my life....

She drained her coffee mug and hooked her finger through the handle so that she could cross her arms. The posture was defensive, and to a man as observant as Mitch it was a dead giveaway, but she didn't care. "You might find it hard to believe, considering how I was raised, but I'm happy here, Mitch. This place fills..." She paused, searching for the right word. An emptiness? A need?

Yet why was she trying to explain anything to him?

Was she actually about to open her heart again, fall into the old pattern simply because he was here? Maybe she hadn't changed that much after all. It was an alarming thought. "It keeps me busy," she finished. She turned. "Speaking of which, I have some paperwork I need to catch up on."

He touched her arm to stop her from moving away. "Are you expecting anyone else, Chantal?"

Even though her jacket, a sweater and a blouse separated her skin from his hand, she imagined she could feel his touch all the way to her toes. Her determination to remain cool dissolved. She jerked sideways to break the contact.

He dropped his arm fast and stepped back, as if he were as determined as she was to reestablish the distance between them.

Terrific. That pattern hadn't appeared to have changed, either. She cleared her throat. "Excuse me?"

"Any other guests."

"No. The Petherick Corporation has exclusive use of the place until next weekend. Why?"

He pointed to the west. "I hear a chopper."

All she could hear was the rhythm of her pulse in her ears. "The mist can distort sound," she said.

"It's coming in fast. Not over the lake, either."

She tipped her head. Though the mist still clung to the water, the sky overhead was clear. She heard the beat of the engine now. It was getting louder quickly. That was odd. Aircraft not connected with the resort did fly past from time to time, yet she'd never seen any this early in the day. She'd checked her e-mail through the resort's satellite computer hookup as soon as she'd gotten up this morning, and there had been no message about any visitors. "It could be heading for the state park," she said, starting back toward the staircase. "There might be a lost hiker. I'll check the radio when I get in."

"I noticed my cell phone doesn't get a signal out here," he said, falling into step beside her. "Is the radio your primary source of communication?"

"For some things. I do most of my business over e-mail. If there's someone you absolutely need to contact, you can access the Internet through the computer in my office, but very few of my guests use it. Our isolation is one of our main selling features. It provides a true getaway vacation."

"How do you get your supplies in?"

"By truck. There's an old logging road that connects to the main road from Bethel Corners."

"That's the nearest community? Bethel Corners?"

"Yes, but the route's too rough for anything without a four-wheel drive. Our guests prefer to come by air. It's faster and more comfortable."

He glanced toward the noise of the helicopter. It continued to get louder. "But you wouldn't have any drop-ins."

"No. Our business is strictly by reservation."

There was a roar overhead as the helicopter cleared the hill behind the lodge. It exposed a dull, black underside before it swung out of sight once more. It definitely wasn't from the park service. And it appeared to be landing.

She started up the staircase. "Well, whoever that is, they've no doubt woken the other guests. Please, stay here and enjoy the rest of your coffee."

He tipped his mug to empty it and followed her. "I think I'll tag along. Something's not right. That chopper didn't have any markings."

"Really, Mitch," she said, raising her voice over the noise. "I'm sure there's no cause for worry."

He didn't look convinced. "Just be careful."

Pride had her wanting to reject his caution. He didn't care. She knew better than to imagine he did. Still, she was getting a bad feeling about the unscheduled visitors, too. The sound of the engine wound down gradually as she and Mitch climbed. They were halfway up when Chantal heard what sounded like a muffled scream.

It had to have been a seagull, she told herself. The cries they made when they wheeled above the lake could sound hauntingly human. And the water had a way of amplifying sound when the air was calm like this, so the bird could be miles away.

But her steps faltered anyway. Behind her, she sensed that Mitch did the same. An instant later, there was another scream. It was unmistakable, even over the waning noise of the helicopter. It was followed by a burst of rapid pops.

Chantal couldn't quite process what she was hearing. This was the Aerie. It was her sanctuary. Nothing bad happened here.

That couldn't be…gunfire, could it?

Mitch grabbed her wrist and yanked her to a halt. "Stop!" he ordered. "We need to take cover."

The look on his face confirmed what she didn't want to believe. It *was* real. Someone was shooting. It wasn't the measured cracks of a hunting rifle but the stuttering taps of a machine gun. "This can't be! Who—"

"We're too exposed here." He turned and started back down, tugging her behind him. "We have to get off the stairs."

She stumbled downward a few steps before she managed to pull loose from his grip. "No! Someone could be hurt! I have to see—"

"Chantal, whatever's happening up there, we won't be

able to do much against automatic weapons when we're armed with nothing but a pair of coffee cups."

She glanced at her hand. Somehow, she was still clutching her mug.

"Until we see what's going on, the best way to help is not to get shot." He took the mug from her fingers. "Is there another route up?"

As much as she hated following orders from any man, and especially from *this* one, she recognized this wasn't the time for discussion. "There's a path behind the boathouse," she said, reversing direction. "Follow me."

By the time they reached the outcrop that held the lodge, the noise of the helicopter had wound down to silence. So had the gunfire. Mitch didn't consider either fact encouraging: whoever had done the shooting had accomplished what they'd wanted and were planning to stay a while.

He directed Chantal toward the side of the building opposite the deck and staircase, where the slope of the hill was less steep, then pulled her to a halt behind a group of boulders and pantomimed an order for her to stay put. He flattened himself on the ground. Using his knees and elbows, he dragged himself across the rock toward a patch of low-growing junipers. With the evergreen branches as cover, he cautiously raised his head.

He found he was looking through a side window into the lobby. The rising sun streamed through the glass wall at the front like a searchlight. In spite of the narrow angle of Mitch's view, he could see a large section of the interior. Movement on the second-floor gallery caught his eye first. Graham was being herded down the curving staircase to the lobby by a man wearing a black balaclava and carrying a submachine gun. Another masked gunman stood beside the fireplace where the four Petherick executives were sitting in a group on the wooden floor, their hands clasped on their heads.

Whoever these intruders were, it seemed they had caught everyone in their beds. No one had had the time to get dressed. Graham had managed to throw a robe over his pajamas, but his feet were bare. Jim Whitby, the Petherick Corporation comptroller, was in his underwear. The research director was in a jogging suit. The two women vice presidents were huddled together, sharing a blanket across their shoulders. They were both sobbing.

Pebbles gritted against the rock near his feet. Mitch turned his head in time to see Chantal creep toward him. He frowned and gestured for her to go back.

She shook her head quickly and lay on her stomach beside him. Her eyes widened as she focused on the window.

Mitch shifted closer until his shoulder pressed against hers. He could feel her tension through her jacket. The Chantal he used to know would have been in tears by now. She'd never been much good at controlling her emotions or her impulses. He could only hope the new version wouldn't fall apart.

"This has to be a mistake," she whispered.

He put his mouth close to her ear, keeping his reply as quiet as hers. "That chopper couldn't have landed here by accident. This attack must have been planned."

"But why? There's nothing of value here to steal."

Mitch focused on the gunmen. From here it looked as if they carried AK47s, which were cheap and relatively easy to come by, making them the terrorist's firearm of choice. The men appeared comfortable with their weapons. Their movements were purposeful, not frantic. "These guys don't look like amateurs. I don't think this is a simple robbery. No one would go to this much trouble for credit cards and a few laptops and Rolexes."

"Then what?"

Good question. He watched as the three army officers were ushered at gunpoint down to the lobby by a third gunman. The general was in striped pajamas but the others had managed to throw on their clothes before they'd been taken. Someone had used plastic bundling ties to bind their hands, a quick and effective technique that Mitch's own men had been trained to use. If these officers had attempted to resist, they couldn't have tried too hard. Like the others, they didn't appear to be injured. They were pushed roughly toward Graham's people.

Chantal angled her head farther to her right. "I don't see any of my staff."

"Where would they be?"

"Our rooms are behind the kitchen."

"Is there an exit nearby?"

"At the back. Maybe they got out before—" She sucked in her breath at a flurry of movement from beneath the gallery. "Oh, no. Henry."

A lanky boy who couldn't have been much more than twelve ran across the lobby. One of the gunmen grabbed the back of his pajamas as he passed and jerked him to a stop. The boy squirmed in his grip and landed a kick to his shin. The man gave him a shake that snapped his head back on his thin neck.

Chantal swore and started to rise.

Mitch slung his arm around her back and used it to press her to the ground. "Don't."

She turned her face toward his. "But he's just a child. He's terrified. I have to—"

"What? Run in there and get caught like the rest of them? That's not going to help."

Her cheeks flushed. Her lips moved as if she were biting back a protest.

He understood how she felt. It was taking a tremendous amount of self-control to watch and do nothing. "Mounting a direct assault against an unknown number of armed hostiles would be futile at best, suicidal at worst," he said. "So far I've seen three intruders. All armed. That chopper they arrived in could have carried four times that number, so it's a safe bet there are a few more someplace. This is no time to give in to your emotions. We need to use our heads."

Briefly she seemed about to argue further, but then she returned her attention to the window.

A short woman raced toward the boy. She yanked the child from the gunman's grip and clasped him in her arms, as if she could shelter him with her body.

"His mother?" Mitch asked.

"Tyra Pearson. She's my assistant manager. Her husband's the cook. They're like family to me. They're… Oh, *God*. Walter's hurt."

A plump, blond man was pushed from the shadows beneath the gallery by a fourth gunman. He staggered toward the woman and child. Blood darkened his forehead and the right side of his face.

Mitch guessed even before Chantal told him that this was the boy's father. Obviously, the man had tried to defend his family and had been struck for his efforts. There was no way to tell for certain from here how serious the injury was. From the look of it, Mitch guessed he'd been pistol-whipped rather than shot.

The young couple who had helped carry the guests' luggage the night before were the last to be brought in. Their resemblance to each other was more obvious than it had been yesterday—they must be brother and sister.

Neither attempted any heroics. They moved like people in shock.

At least they were able to move. Considering all the rounds that he'd heard fired earlier, Mitch had been prepared to see far worse. "Is that everyone?" he whispered. "All your staff?"

"Yes."

"Then aside from Walter, no one's been harmed. It looks as if they wanted hostages."

"Hostages?"

"Altogether they've got thirteen. They've assembled everyone in one place to make it easier to keep track of them."

"Why? What could they want?"

"At this stage, all that matters is that they want everyone alive." *For now,* he added silently. The fact the gunmen were all masked could indicate they meant to leave survivors.

Or it could mean they simply wanted to intimidate their captives. Not being able to see an attacker's face was bound to instill fear. It was another technique familiar to Eagle Squadron—they often donned masks themselves when executing a raid. "Our priority is to get help before someone matches the number of people to the number of beds and realizes they're two short."

A tall man with a chest like a barrel appeared at the gallery railing. He seemed to be giving orders to the others, so evidently, this was the leader. Like the rest of the men, his face was concealed by a balaclava. Only his air of command distinguished him from the others. That, and the sidearm he wore at his waist. He spoke into a handheld walkie-talkie as he surveyed the room, then suddenly turned his head to look out the side window.

Mitch splayed his hand, gently increasing the pressure on Chantal's back. "Don't move," he breathed.

She began to tremble. "Oh, God. He's looking straight at us."

"We've got the junipers in front of us and the sun's in his face. He probably can't see much against the glare. Stay down and we'll be fine."

"What are we going to do if he does see us?"

"We'll use an old army trick."

"What?"

"We run like hell."

Her breath hitched. "I hate the army."

"You? A general's daughter?"

"Never knew that, did you."

He suspected there were plenty of things he didn't know about Chantal, both the old and the new versions.

Except, surprisingly, she still smelled the same. Even with the scents of rock, lichen and evergreens that surrounded them, he could pick hers out. Roses. It was old-fashioned. Feminine. He'd never been able to smell it without remembering a rainy, October night and the touch of soft flesh…

Mitch gave himself a mental shake. What the hell was he thinking? He lifted his hand from Chantal's back. "Okay, he's looking the other way. Slide back to those boulders."

"Then what?"

"Then we find a way to—"

Gunfire blasted from behind them. Mitch automatically cupped the back of Chantal's head and pushed her face into his shoulder, giving her what protection he could. He felt rather than heard her cry out as bullets *pinged* from the rock beside them.

The firing ended as quickly as it had begun. A man spoke into the sudden silence. “Got ’em, Knox!”

Chapter 3

Chantal sensed that Mitch was trying to tell her something, even though he hadn't spoken a word since he'd gotten to his feet. She could see it in the set of his jaw and the tightening at the corners of his mouth. She could feel it in the tension that radiated from his body as he walked beside her and in the way his eyes gleamed as he glanced toward the trees and then back at her.

Or was this just wishful thinking on her part? She'd once thought they'd had a connection that had transcended the age difference between them. She had misinterpreted the situation then, so she had no reason to think she was any better at reading him now. Simply because he'd been a hero in her teenage imagination didn't mean he actually was one in real life. There was no sign that he was trying to save either one of them. Like her, he was walking with his hands clasped on his head, as he'd been ordered. So far, he'd offered no resistance.

They rounded the corner of the lodge and started toward the rear entrance. The man who'd found them poked his gun into Mitch's back to shove him forward. He'd kept the weapon aimed at him the whole time. Obviously, he didn't consider Chantal any threat. "Come on, keep moving."

Mitch stumbled and knocked against her. He mumbled what sounded like an apology.

Chantal could feel a scream building. From frustration, from fear. From the sheer wrongness of what was happening. He'd said they needed to use their heads, and she understood that. Yet her heart rebelled at the idea of giving up so easily. They were steps from the back door, seconds away from being herded like sheep to join the rest of the hostages.

She looked over her shoulder at their captor. He was a huge man, built like an oversized fire hydrant. The black knit fabric that covered his face had a round hole for his mouth and an oblong slit for his eyes. It took away his humanity, making him seem like something out of a horror movie or a nightmare...or news footage of terrorists.

The urge to scream strengthened.

No. She wasn't going to give in to hysteria. This was her home. Her staff was her family, and her guests were her responsibility. They depended on her; she had to be strong.

And dammit, she would not allow herself to be a victim. "Who are you people?" she asked, slowing her steps.

"Shut up and keep moving."

"Not until you give me some answers. I'm the manager here. I demand to know what's going on."

"I said shut up."

She halted and turned to face him. "Why did you come here? What do you want?"

Behind the round mouth-hole, his lips twisted. "Get going. Now."

She dropped her hands and lifted her chin. "Whatever you planned, you're not going to get away with it. You have no right—"

"Lady, you're really starting to piss me off," he said, swinging the gun away from Mitch.

The instant the gun barrel was no longer pressed to his back, Mitch exploded into action. He pivoted, swinging his bent arm backward so quickly it was a blur. There was a thudding crunch as his elbow connected with their captor's windpipe.

The man dropped his gun and clawed at his throat, gasping for air.

Mitch drove his fist into his temple.

The man crumpled to the ground and lay motionless.

Stooping fast, Mitch grabbed the gun then snatched the man's walkie-talkie and tossed it to Chantal. "Which way to your truck?"

"My truck?"

He patted the man's pockets, withdrew all the spare ammunition clips and stuffed them into his own pockets. "You said you drive your supplies here." He straightened. "Show me where you keep your vehicles."

She looked at the downed man. He still hadn't stirred. "Is he…"

"His larynx is crushed. He'll be more of a drain on their resources if he's disabled rather than dead." Mitch grasped her arm and turned her away. "But we're going to have about thirty seconds before someone comes looking for him. We need to go now, Chantal."

She clutched the walkie-talkie tightly in her hands. Mitch's burst of violence had shaken her almost as much as their sudden freedom. "But you have his gun. Can't we do something?"

"Not alone. Without a coordinated assault there's too much risk to the hostages." He gave her a nudge to start her moving. "We need to get reinforcements."

After one last glance at the Aerie—and a quick prayer for the people left inside—she plunged through a gap in the trees.

Mitch stayed right behind her. They weren't hampered by the need for stealth this time. In less than a minute they reached the three-sided drive shed where the vehicles were kept.

Chantal wrenched open the door of her four-wheel-drive pickup truck and slid behind the wheel. As usual, the keys were in the ignition. The need for convenience had always outweighed the need for security here at the Aerie. She'd never dreamed her habit would prove an advantage when she was fleeing for her life.

She dropped the walkie-talkie on the floor, fastened her seat belt and cranked the engine.

A gunshot cracked through the shed.

She cringed reflexively, then whipped her head around to look for Mitch.

Thank God, he was the only one doing the shooting. He was jogging past the other vehicles, firing methodically at the tires. Within seconds the Pearsons' SUV, Rhonda and Tommy's Jeep and the resort's four all-terrain vehicles were settling onto the rims of their wheels.

She barely had time to absorb the destruction when the passenger door flew open and Mitch jumped inside. "Go!" he yelled.

Chantal gripped the wheel and aimed for the track that led down the hill. She took the first bend too fast and slid sideways. Spruce boughs screeched along the fender before she regained control.

Mitch propped the gun between his feet. "Who's your nearest neighbor?"

He sounded so calm. As if he did this kind of thing all the time. Then again, he probably did. She swallowed hard and tried to match his tone. "Waterfalls Resort. It's an outfitter's camp at the north end of the lake. They're closed for the season, but the owner would still be there."

"I assume they would have a radio?"

"Yes."

"We'll have to head there."

"That's what I'm doing."

"How far is it?"

"At this rate, maybe an hour."

"You told me the lake was only sixteen miles long."

"As the crow flies. With the twists of the road, it's more than double that. I need to head west before I can take the fork to the north, but it's still faster than driving to Bethel Corners."

He retrieved the gun, pulled out the magazine to check the ammunition, then snapped it back into place.

"You were trying to give us a head start," she said. "That's why you shot out those tires."

"Right. Hopefully, Knox and his gang will waste some time before they figure out they can't follow by land."

"Knox? Did you recognize those men?"

"No. That's the name the guy who caught us said into his walkie-talkie. It's probably their leader." He twisted to look behind them. "It's going to take them several minutes to get their chopper back in the air. We need to be as far away as we can by then."

"I understand that."

"You're going to need to go faster."

"Not if I don't want to roll us."

"Pull over. I'll drive."

"No."

"Chantal—"

"I know this road. I know this truck. You don't." She steered around an exposed boulder and gunned the engine at the top of a small rise. They went airborne for a second, splashed through a puddle and accelerated out of the next turn.

Mitch braced one hand on the dashboard to help steady himself. "You're not a bad driver."

"You'd better not say, 'for a woman.'"

"I wouldn't dream of it. I was thinking you're good for a civilian."

"Gee, thanks."

"Where's the walkie-talkie I liberated?" he asked.

"On the floor at my feet."

He leaned over her lap. "I see it," he muttered, stretching his arm between her legs. His chest pressed into her thigh. The back of his head brushed her right breast.

She gripped the wheel hard, concentrating on keeping the truck steady. She didn't want even to think what would happen if they hit a bump while they were in this position. She didn't want to think about the position, either. This body contact wasn't personal, she reminded herself. Regardless of how personal it felt.

His arm rubbed across her calf as he groped along the floor. He straightened, the walkie-talkie in his hand, and sat back. "Got it."

She let out her breath. She hadn't realized she'd been holding it. She pressed down on the gas and skidded into the next turn. "Can we call out on that thing?"

He inspected it before he replied. "No, this model has preset frequencies and a limited range. We can only listen.

It should give us an idea of what they're up to." The hiss of static filled the cab. No voices. Mitch fiddled with the controls. "By the way, that was a nice diversion back there."

"What diversion?"

"When you drew the guy's attention. I wasn't sure you got my message."

She risked a glance at him. "I wasn't sure you were sending me one. I had thought you'd given up."

"I didn't want to make a move while we were still within sight of their leader. He was watching through the side window."

"Ah. That makes sense."

"And I never give up without a fight. You should have had some faith in me, Chantal."

"I'm not in the habit of waiting to be rescued, Mitch."

"I'm a soldier. This is what I'm trained for."

"Regardless, I've found it's easier not to depend on anyone."

"Until this is over, we're going to have to depend on each other."

"I suppose we will."

He met her gaze. "Regardless of our history."

The truck lurched into a pothole hard enough to jar her teeth. She looked away from him to focus on her driving. "Our history," she repeated. "This is hardly the time to get into that, is it?"

"It's exactly the time. A team never functions at its best if there's tension between the members."

"Maybe having my home invaded by a pack of armed thugs, seeing my friends terrorized, getting shot at and fleeing for my life before I've had a chance to digest my breakfast explains any tension you might be sensing here.

Don't flatter yourself by assuming you're the cause, Mitch. I got over you a long time ago."

"I'm sure you did."

"I grew up."

"I noticed."

"So there's no reason to dredge up the past. Besides, I thought we'd already settled this when we were out on the dock."

"You don't really think I bought that polite act of yours, do you?"

"What act?"

"Your body language didn't match your words. There was plenty more you wanted to say on the subject of our past."

Her knuckles were white where she gripped the wheel. She flexed her fingers. "You're the one who brought this up, so maybe you're the one with more to say."

"True enough."

"Although, I can't imagine what. You made yourself crystal clear seventeen years ago."

"Yes, and I've owed you an apology since then."

They had entered a pine grove. The rising sun was casting deep bars of shadow across the road, which hampered her depth perception. Chantal didn't want to slow down, but she needed to or risk tearing out the oil pan on a rock. She eased off the gas and leaned closer to the windshield.

It wasn't cowardice that kept her focus on the road. It was necessity. Or so she told herself. Damn him.

He touched his fingers to her arm. "I *am* sorry, Chantal."

She concentrated on her driving. She wouldn't permit herself to look at him, because she was sure she'd heard a roughness in his voice. And she wasn't going to be foolish enough to believe it was from emotion. It was from the bumpy road.

"If you're saying those words only because you believe it would make us a more efficient team," she said, "then don't bother."

He dropped his hand to his lap. "You're not giving me an inch, are you?"

Why should she? she thought. The last time she'd offered him anything, he'd turned her down. He'd thrown a blanket over her and had run for the door.

"I'm sorry we parted the way we did," he said. "I should have been more understanding. Your mother had just died. I should have known you had only wanted comfort."

No, I'd wanted love, *Mitch. I wanted you to be my first and my only lover. I would have gladly given you my trust, my heart and my virginity if only you would have loved me....*

She spoke through her teeth. "Don't patronize me."

"I didn't then and I'm not now. You're no longer a child so you must be able to understand the reality of the situation. You were my commanding officer's teenage daughter."

"I wasn't a child. I was eighteen."

"You'd had a sheltered life."

God, he was so wrong. "And you were a captain with career ambitions and a convenient sense of honor."

"My honor isn't a convenience. It's the code I live by."

"Then we were a bad mix from the start. I got it then. I get it now."

"Chantal..."

"I can appreciate why you wanted to clear the air, but—"

"Then let me finish. For our sake, and for the sake of

everyone who's being held hostage, we can't let our past hinder us from cooperating."

"Isn't that what we've been doing? Working together?"

"You've been questioning nearly every choice I've made," he pointed out.

"And you think that's because of our history?"

"Isn't it?"

She didn't relax. She couldn't. Yet the edge of a laugh scraped at her throat. "You really don't know me anymore, do you? I'd be questioning anyone. I'm a civilian, not one of the soldiers in your unit. I'm accustomed to making my own choices."

"You have no experience with combat situations."

"You have no experience with this truck, this road or this area."

"Which is why we need to team up."

"Yes, *team* is the operative word. You're not in command here, Major." They emerged from the pine grove into a strip of cleared forest. Only brush and new seedlings grew among the low stumps. Chantal squinted as her eyes adjusted to the sudden sunlight. "If I'd wanted to follow orders, I would have joined—"

A line of dirt and rock chips burst from the track in front of them. Chantal swerved to one side. The truck tilted dangerously as the wheels caught the edge of a rut.

Mitch leaned closer to the windshield and looked up. "It's the chopper."

"They're firing on us!"

"They're smart. They maintained radio silence. They must have guessed I'd be listening."

"Skip the analysis. Do something!"

He was already angling the barrel of his gun out

his window. He fired off several rounds. The noise was deafening but apparently for nothing. The barrage continued uninterrupted.

A shadow fell across the road in front of them. The helicopter hovered above the break in the trees. Its engine was loud enough to drown out Mitch's return fire. Chantal reflexively hit the brakes.

"Speed up," he yelled. "Go under them!"

Or that's what it sounded as if he said. It seemed like the only option. Chantal floored the accelerator. Holes appeared in the hood of the truck. As irrational as it was, she ducked, but no bullets penetrated the cab as they passed beneath the aircraft. In her rearview mirror she saw the landing skids dip and slew as it turned.

"If we can make it to the next line of trees, we'll be back under cover," Mitch said.

Bullets shattered the rear windshield of the pickup then tore through the cargo bed and sides. Gas sprayed into the air as the fuel tank ruptured.

Chantal fought to maintain her grip on the wheel. Mitch twisted backward to fire through the broken windshield. Ahead, the road curved sharply to run parallel to the tree line. It would leave them exposed for another quarter mile. She made a split-second decision, gunned the engine and went straight. "Hang on!" she yelled.

The truck bounced across the ruts and into the cleared strip, missing a ragged stump by inches. Brush dragged at the undercarriage. The trees loomed nearer. Chantal swerved past a sapling and steered toward a gap in the wall of foliage.

Her sudden maneuver took their pursuers by surprise. The gunfire halted for precious seconds as the helicopter swung to realign itself.

But the bullets had already done their damage. Black

smoke billowed from beneath the truck's hood. There was a *whoosh*, and the entire front end was in flames. Chantal shrieked, unable to see, unable to breathe. The truck plowed through a thicket of brush, hit a rock and stopped dead twenty yards from the shelter of the trees.

Mitch opened his door. "We've got to bail before this thing blows!"

Chantal could hear the roar of the helicopter, along with a renewed hail of gunfire. Flames licked across the dashboard, but her hands were shaking so badly she couldn't manage her seat belt. "Mitch!"

He undid the buckle, hooked an arm around her waist and dragged her out from behind the wheel. She felt herself being lifted into the air.

And then, mercifully, she felt nothing at all.

Chapter 4

"Aerie, this is Waterfalls Resort. Come in, please. Over."

Tyra Pearson walked across the manager's office and sat in front of the radio. She fisted her hands in her lap. A voice came over the speaker.

"Chantal, are you there? It's Bob."

Lewis Knox gripped the back of the woman's chair. "Keep it short," he said. "And be convincing."

She nodded. She didn't look at him, she looked at her son.

Taddeo stood in the doorway with a firm grip on the boy. They'd put a strip of duct tape over the kid's mouth to ensure his silence, but seeing his mother cry seemed to have taken the fight out of him. The thin-bladed skinning knife that Taddeo held at his throat wasn't to ensure his cooperation. It was to ensure the mother's.

Lewis had no doubt that she'd do exactly as she'd been told. As always, fear was a good motivator.

Bamford slid the microphone in front of Tyra. At a signal from Lewis, he pressed the switch.

She swallowed, wiped her cheeks with the back of her hand and leaned forward. "Bob, this is Tyra. Over."

"Hey, Tyra! What's going on?"

"Nothing special. Why?"

"I saw black smoke on the horizon a while ago. It looked like it was coming from your area."

"It was nothing to worry about. We have a new group of guests. They wanted a campfire."

"That was some plume of smoke for a campfire. What were they cooking? Old tires?"

"I think someone threw on rotten wood."

"Sounds like you've got your hands full this week."

"What can I say? They're city suits."

"Well, just watch them. The fire hazard's low because of all that rain last month, but if one got out of control we're all in trouble."

"Yes, that's true." She paused. "We hope these guests don't cause us trouble."

Lewis didn't like her tone. It sounded as if she were attempting to send a message. He gestured toward Taddeo.

Taddeo gripped Henry's hair, yanked back his head and flattened the blade of his knife along the boy's neck.

"Henry!" All the blood drained from Tyra's face. She was breathing fast through her mouth. For a second, she looked about ready to pass out.

That wouldn't do them any good. Lewis jerked her chair to get her attention and pointed to the radio.

"Are you okay, Tyra? You're sounding odd."

She gripped the edge of the table. "I'm fine, Bob."

"Something wrong with your boy?"

"No, Henry's fine. I'm just reminding him to do his homework. Only another week and we move back to town. I can't wait."

"Can't wait to get him out of your hair, you mean." He chuckled. "Just make sure those suits don't burn the place down before they leave."

"I'll do my best. I have to go, Bob."

"Okay. Over and out."

Tyra switched off the microphone, leaped from her chair and ran to her son. She yanked him out of Taddeo's grip and held him to her chest, her shoulders shaking.

Bamford rolled the chair that Tyra had used into place behind the manager's desk. "Sounds like he bought it."

As usual, Lewis found Bamford's complacency grating. He looked at Taddeo. "Take them back with the others, then send Hillock and Molitor to me. And you," he said, transferring his attention to Bamford. "I want that computer link set up ASAP."

"No problem." He cracked his knuckles, then set to work at the computer keyboard.

Five minutes later, Lewis was scowling at his helicopter crew. They were too cocky, and he wanted to be sure they saw the displeasure on his face. "Can you guarantee that they're dead?"

"Oh, yeah," Hillock said. He flashed a gap-toothed smile. "The gas tank on that pickup went up like a bomb. They're a pair of crispy critters."

"Did you check?" Lewis persisted.

"We circled around and watched them burn."

"Then you saw two bodies."

Hillock's grin dimmed. "Didn't need to. That truck was a torch. Believe me, they're dead."

"But you didn't land to be certain."

Molitor, the pilot, lifted his beefy shoulders in a shrug. "The area was too rough to set down. I wasn't going to risk hitting the blades on a tree. I took us in as close as I could. Hillock's right. They're toast."

"They had it coming after what they did to Benny," Hillock said.

"Benny Brown got sloppy," Lewis said. "He let them escape."

"It had to be a lucky punch."

Lucky? No, it would have taken considerable skill to get the better of a man the size of Brown. That blow had been meant to crush his throat. Interfering with a man's air supply was the surest way to incapacitate him. It was one of the reasons why Lewis had wanted assurances the person who had done it was dead. Their contact hadn't been able to give him any details about the army men. This one evidently hadn't been a desk jockey.

"You got sloppy, too." Lewis leaned his hips against the edge of the desk and crossed his arms. "You should have shot them instead of causing an explosion and fire."

"Dead is dead, Knox. What difference does it make how we did it?"

"The neighbors spotted the smoke."

Hillock glanced at Molitor, then back at Lewis. "Want us to take them out now?"

Lewis had already considered the idea and rejected it. They had brought enough ordnance to vaporize a small town, but it wasn't yet the time to deploy it. "Not at this stage. We contained the damage, but we can't afford any more mistakes. Go find Walsh and Ferguson. See if they need any help setting the charges."

The men left. Lewis checked his watch, annoyed to see they were already behind schedule. They'd managed to get the situation under control, but they had one man out of commission, they'd lost two potential hostages and had attracted unwanted attention.

They still had a long way to go. This was the kind of unforseen complication that could have derailed his entire plan.

Chantal woke to the warmth of sunlight on her face. That was odd. She never overslept. Yet for the moment she was content to drift in the remnants of her dream. She was enveloped by the scent of leather and...Mitch.

That was strange, too. She'd stopped dreaming of Mitch years ago, yet the sensation of his presence was so real, so intimate, she felt as if his arms were around her....

A crow squawked above her. Chantal blinked.

She wasn't in her bed. She wasn't in Mitch's embrace. She was lying on the ground at the base of a maple tree.

Full awareness surged over her. Her pulse tripped as images collided in her head. The helicopter. The fire. "Mitch!" she cried, pushing herself to her elbows.

The crow took off. Wind rustled the leaves overhead. Other than that, Chantal could see no movement. She tried to stand, but a spurt of dizziness made her sit down fast. She braced her hands on her knees. She had to breathe deeply a few times before she attempted to lift her head again.

She was at the edge of a small open space in the forest. A short distance away, a shallow stream burbled over rounded rocks. She didn't recognize where she was or remember how she got here. The sound of the helicopter was completely gone. How long had she been unconscious? Had she been wandering in a daze? The last thing she remembered clearly were the flames that had stretched toward Mitch's face.

Mitch! Where was he? Was he all right? She got to

her knees, crawled closer to the maple and used the trunk to pull herself up. The movement brought on a fierce pounding at the back of her skull. She waited until the pain receded then took a more thorough look at her surroundings.

That's when she spotted Mitch's jacket. She'd been lying on it. The gun he'd been using was propped on a moss-covered log a few yards beyond that. A hazy memory rose in her mind: a hard shoulder pressing into her stomach, leather rubbing against her cheek while the ground moved past upside down beneath her.

Mitch must have carried her. He'd brought her here. That meant he was all right. He'd pulled her from the truck and had taken care of her, in spite of how she'd been snapping at him earlier.

She leaned her forehead against the tree, swamped by a wave of remorse. There had been a time when she'd convinced herself she hated Mitch. She'd wished he would drop off the face of the earth. That attitude had come from her wounded pride and from a desire to find someone else to blame besides herself for the mess her life had become. She'd never truly wished him harm. She knew he was a good man. An honorable man. If he hadn't been, she wouldn't have fallen in love with him so thoroughly.

And if he hadn't been so honorable, he wouldn't have rejected her.

That was one aspect of their history that even now she didn't like to consider. It would mean that her love for him had been doomed from the start. It would also mean the resentment she'd harbored wasn't justified.

He'd tried to apologize, yet she'd thrown it back in his face. Considering the circumstances, that seemed like an incredibly petty thing to have done.

But if not for the circumstances, would he have apologized?

God, what did any of that matter? They'd been shot at. Her truck had blown up. They could have been killed.

"Chantal?"

She lifted her head and turned in the direction of his voice.

He was moving toward her, his steps uneven. He leaned heavily on a stout branch that he was using as a cane.

She shoved away from the tree and staggered to meet him. "Mitch!"

He dropped the branch and grabbed her arms to steady her. "Hey, careful. Don't move so fast."

"What's wrong? You're limping!"

"I twisted my ankle. It's not serious." He studied her. "I'm glad to see you're awake. How are you feeling?"

"Fine. Mitch—"

"Any dizziness?" He took her chin in one hand and peered into her eyes, then tilted her face toward the sun and did the same. "Headache?"

"A little."

"You probably have a concussion. You were out a long time."

"What happened?"

"What do you remember?"

"I remember you pulling me out of the truck before it exploded."

"We landed in a patch of brush when the truck blew. The leaves and the smoke screened us from the guys in the chopper. I waited until they left and then carried you here."

His account was military-terse, only the facts. Most other men would be boasting about their heroism. "Thank you, Mitch. I owe you my life."

"I might have made your headache worse by moving you. We had to get out of sight in case the helicopter returned for another sweep." He stroked her hair from her forehead and tucked it behind her ears. His hand lingered at the side of her neck. "We're safe here. You should stay put for a while until you feel steadier."

"Don't worry about me. You're the one who must be in pain. You carried me on a twisted ankle."

"You're not that heavy. Besides, we're a team, remember?"

She pulled back to get a better look at him. His right cheek and the side of his jaw bore shallow scratches, possibly from the brush they'd landed in. His gray sweatshirt had a small rip at the neckline and was streaked with dirt and what appeared to be soot. It was a Patriots sweatshirt. He'd always been a New England fan. He'd been watching football the last night she'd seen him. The TV had been droning in the background when she'd called to beg him to come....

She didn't know why she was remembering such a meaningless detail after what they'd just been through.

And she really didn't know why she had this completely insane urge to kiss him. He looked wonderful to her, despite the dirt and the scratches. He'd always been appealing in a uniform, but he seemed even more handsome like this. Messy, fresh from a fight. A born warrior, he thrived on challenge. It put a special gleam in his eyes that any female, regardless of age, couldn't fail to notice.

Damn. Her feelings for him *were* over, weren't they?

She turned away more quickly than she should have. That aggravated the pounding in her head. She had to take a few sideways steps to regain her balance.

Mitch moved behind her and clamped his arm around her waist. "Careful. The ground's uneven."

Her back was pressed to his chest. She could feel his voice beside her ear. His warmth, his scent, once more enveloped her. For an instant she wanted to melt into his embrace, but of course, she knew it wasn't meant as an embrace. It was as impersonal as all the other body contact they'd shared today. She gripped his arm and did her best to ignore the rock-hard muscle beneath his sleeve. "Thanks."

"Can you make it as far as the log where I left my gun?"

At her nod, he released her long enough to retrieve the branch he'd dropped, then kept one arm around her as he guided her toward the log. Once she was seated, he hobbled to the stream. "You did well back there, Chantal," he said. "Another few seconds and we would have made those trees."

She rubbed her forehead. "I don't know how I managed to drive. My hands were shaking. I could hardly feel the wheel."

"There's a guy in my unit named Lang who could learn some evasive driving tips from you."

"Knowing the caliber of soldiers who get chosen for Delta Force, I find that hard to believe. You don't need to bend the truth in order to make me feel better."

Mitch sat on a rounded rock at the edge of the stream. He was wearing low hiking boots. He leaned down to unlace the left one. "Okay. You're right about my men. Any one of them could drive doughnuts around you, but that doesn't mean you're a bad driver. That just means they're extraordinary men."

How typical of Mitch. He'd boast about his unit but not about himself. "How far off the road are we?" she asked.

"It's around half a klick that way," he said, pointing his thumb back the way he'd come.

"Half a kilometer! Your ankle—"

"Stop worrying about it. I've had worse." He eased off his boot, then pulled off his sock and thrust his foot into the water. His back was toward her, so she couldn't see his face, yet she heard the grimace in his voice. "Cripes, that water's cold."

"Are you hoping to numb your ankle?"

"That, and take down the swelling."

She watched him for a while, then tugged off her jacket and her sweater. Mitch still had his back to her, so she took off her blouse and quickly put the sweater back on. "Here," she said, wadding the blouse into a ball. She lobbed it toward him. "Use this."

He looked over his shoulder, then stretched to pick up the crumpled cotton. He regarded it, then her. "What's this for?"

"I took some emergency first aid courses when I started managing the Aerie. I remember enough of them to know your ankle should be wrapped to give the joint support."

"I'll lace my boot tighter."

"Use the blouse, too. It has long sleeves, so there's a fair amount of fabric. You could rip it into strips and fasten them together. It's worth a try."

"You shouldn't be sacrificing your clothing for me."

"It's not a sacrifice. I always dress in layers at this time of year. And I thought this team thing works both ways."

He slid his palm over the blouse. His nostrils flared, as if he were inhaling. "Okay. Thanks."

"You're welcome. I hope it helps."

"By the time your headache starts to lift, I should be good to go."

"We no longer have any transportation."

"It's true we've had a minor setback—"

"Minor? We were almost killed!"

"But we weren't. And we now have an advantage."

"We do?"

"While you were out, I went back to see if I could salvage anything from what's left of the truck." He folded the blouse and draped it over his discarded boot, then raised one side of his sweatshirt. The walkie-talkie he'd taken from the guard was strapped to his belt at his hip. "I found it embedded in a rotten stump. It still works."

"That's good."

"There's more. From what I was able to hear, Knox and his gang believe we're dead. That means they won't be looking for us."

"What about my friends? And the guests? Are they still all right?"

There was a trace of discomfort in his expression. He turned back to the stream. "No one's been harmed."

"What aren't you telling me? Did you hear anything else?"

"Enough to know Knox has a timetable. It's imperative that we get help."

She focused on Mitch's improvised cane. Knowing him, he'd be stubborn enough to attempt the walk to Waterfalls on his injured ankle, but it would be excruciating. She pushed herself to her feet. Though the pain in her skull made her squint, she tried to tell herself it was milder than before. "I'll go."

"Where?"

"The other end of the lake. If I get started now—"

"Out of the question." He pulled his foot out of the

water, grabbed his cane and was standing before her in an instant. "I'm not letting you go anywhere on your own."

"You won't *let* me? I thought I already reminded you that I'm not one of your men."

He held up his palm. "Poor choice of word. It's safer if we stay together, but walking to that other resort is no longer our best option."

"Do you have a better one?"

"No, you do. You have a boat. A mahogany launch, if I remember correctly."

"Yes, but it's at the Aerie."

"That's why we need to go back."

Her first reaction was to reject the idea. It was crazy. They'd barely escaped with their lives.

"Knox's people think we're dead," he went on. "So they'll probably be concentrating their attention on the hostages they have. They can't see the boathouse from the lodge. If we wait until dark, we should be able to get the boat onto the lake without detection."

"They'd hear the motor."

"Not if we paddle it far enough and then keep it at low throttle."

She rubbed her hand against her leg. He made it sound easy. He was deliberately downplaying the risk. There were countless things that could go wrong, yet what other choice did they have? "We don't have to go back by the road," she said. "There's a hiking trail that runs along the base of the hill, closer to the lake. It's shorter."

"Then we're agreed."

"Yes, I guess we are."

"Great." Mitch touched his index finger to her chin. "And for the record, I could never confuse you with one of my men, Chantal. They wouldn't dare to question my orders." He moved his finger to her lip. "Not as often or as openly as you do, anyway."

In spite of the headache, pleasure zinged through her heightened nerves. Beneath his touch, her lip throbbed. And just like that, the urge to kiss him returned.

It was the situation, she told herself. Her emotions were raw. This urge had to be the result of some primitive, physical reaction to the excitement of their escape. It meant nothing. She tipped her head, breaking the contact. "And that's the only difference?" she asked.

He was still looking at her mouth. "Hell, no."

She could feel his gaze as vividly as she'd felt his touch. In spite of what she'd just told herself, the pleasure spread.

"You've become a beautiful woman, Chantal. You didn't really think I hadn't noticed, did you?"

Deep inside, the girl she used to be pumped her arms in the air and did a twirl of triumph. There was a time when she would have given anything to get a compliment like that from Mitch and to see the interest in his eyes.

But that was all the more reason she shouldn't believe what she saw or trust what she felt. Too many echoes from the past remained. Sunlight glinted from his wedding band. The noise of the stream beyond him sounded like distant laughter. "I would never presume to guess what you notice about me, Mitch, or what you think. We both know I was dead wrong before."

"Chantal..."

"So thank you for the compliment, but considering what you called our history, and the problems we need to deal with right now, I don't think this is a topic we should pursue."

Chapter 5

The wind died with the approach of dusk, leaving the lake as smooth as glass. A loon was calling again. Its plaintive cry echoed across the water and reflected from the rock slope beneath the Aerie. Though the lodge was hidden by the trees and the curve of the hill, the next bend in the trail gave Mitch an unobstructed view of the boathouse. He halted to study it.

Like the other buildings he'd seen here, it had been constructed of logs, except the ones used on the boathouse were smaller in circumference and aligned vertically instead of horizontally. It was roughly square, with two windows on each side, a pair of double doors like a garage in the front and one man-door at the back. The limited access points would have made it a potential trap, if not for the fact it sat over the water.

"Is there electricity in the boathouse?" Mitch asked.

"I don't remember seeing any cable running down the hill."

Chantal moved beside him. A layer of pine needles muffled her footsteps. "There are solar panels on the roof," she said. "They're enough to power the lights and the cooler, but there's less chance of being seen if we use flashlights."

"Hang on. Did you say 'cooler?' As in food?"

"As in bait. Night crawlers and minnows." She paused. "You and your men might be trained to live off the land and subsist on grubs and such, but I'll hold out until we get to Waterfalls."

He heartily agreed, although the prospect of getting a square meal was fast becoming as urgent as getting help. He and Chantal had found berries and plenty of clean water to keep up their energy during the day, yet without proper nourishment, they would start losing their strength as well as their judgment. "Where are the flashlights?"

"There's an equipment cabinet inside the boathouse. That's where we store life vests and other boating supplies. There should be a few Maglights in there."

"In that case, we'll be able to wait until full dark before we go in. That's good. It'll give us a chance to make sure the place is empty."

"You said they wouldn't be expecting us. They think we're dead."

"It never hurts to be careful. If I were in command up there," he said, gesturing toward the top of the hill, "I wouldn't be taking anything for granted." He leaned his back against a tree at the side of the trail so he could shift his weight to his right leg. "How's your head?"

"Better. How's your ankle?"

Rather than lie, he shrugged. The ankle hurt like hell, but it would have been a lot worse if not for the improvised wrap Chantal had provided. It hadn't helped in the way she'd intended, though. The blouse hadn't yielded enough fabric to give much support to the joint. Its chief benefit was as a distraction.

The garment had been against Chantal's skin. It had still carried her scent and the warmth of her body when she'd given it to him. So instead of being aware of the pain with each step he took, he found himself thinking about where the blouse had been. And how she had stripped in his presence. What would have happened if he'd turned his head at that moment? What would he have seen?

He'd already noticed that her breasts were larger than they used to be. The years had added fullness. Was her skin still as creamy? Were her nipples still as pink?

The image of the night he and Chantal had parted flashed through his mind. Again. He clenched his teeth and shoved it away. He had no business remembering those details. It was sick. She'd been a kid.

That's what he used to tell himself, anyway. It hadn't been entirely accurate. As she'd reminded him already, she'd been eighteen the last time he'd seen her. She might have had the innocence of a girl, but it had been damn hard to view her like one when she'd been naked.

There was no question that she was all woman now. Had she felt the same spark of chemistry that he had back there by the stream? Or had he read those looks on her face wrong?

"Are you sure you're all right? You seem in pain."

He had to find a better way to distract himself. If his thoughts continued in this direction, he'd have a whole different problem. "I'm fine."

"I can get the launch out on my own and pick you up here."

"I said I'm fine."

She stepped closer. "You might want to keep your voice down. Sound can travel for miles over water on an evening like this."

Mitch rubbed his face, squeezing his jaw until the scratches on it stung. What the hell was wrong with him? How many times had he warned his men not to let their personal feelings get involved when they were on a mission? He'd never imagined he'd be reminding himself. Granted, this might not be an official mission, but he had to approach it that way. Regardless of how attractive he found his teammate, he had to keep a clear head and remember his priorities. Their lives could depend on it. "How are you with guns?" he asked.

"What do you mean?"

He unslung the AK47 from his shoulder and held it out to her. "Ever used one of these?"

Chantal made no move to take it. "What? No!"

"It's a relatively simple weapon. See this lever on the side?" He turned the right side toward her. "It's a combination safety and fire selector."

"Why are you showing me?"

"You need to know how to use this in case I can't."

"Well, that had better not happen because I could never shoot anyone."

"You'd be surprised what you're capable of when your life's at stake." He took her hand and placed it beneath the stock of the gun. "Here."

She flexed her fingers under his. "There's no point."

"If you handle it as if you know what you're doing, that might be enough. You might never need to fire it." He took her other hand and put it over the safety. "First step, memorize where this is."

She held herself stiffly. He could see the revulsion on her face and something more, a trace of real fear. It took her a while before she was willing to grasp the weapon herself. Her arms dipped. "It's heavier than it looks," she said.

It was almost nine pounds. Twice as much as the M16s his men preferred to use. "Try lifting it to your shoulder."

She did as he instructed. She winced as the strap caught a lock of her hair.

He helped her ease it loose, then showed her how to hold the pistol grip and directed the barrel of the gun toward the ground. "Important lesson: only point at what you intend to shoot."

"I've always hated guns, Mitch. I really don't think I can do this."

"Look at it as a tool. It won't do anything without your consent. You're the one in charge. Now, where's the safety?"

She seemed as if she wanted to protest again, but practicality apparently won. She tilted the gun to the side and set her fingers where he'd shown her.

"Right." He put his hand over hers again and guided her through the motions. "All the way up means it's safe. One notch down means full automatic fire." He moved the lever down, then down again. "The bottom position is single shot, but you'd be better off keeping it on automatic. It can fire ten rounds a second, so as long as you do a steady sweep you're bound to hit what you're aiming at."

She shuddered. "Are you done?"

"Not yet." He returned the lever to the top setting then moved her fingers to the trigger. "Do you feel that? It's directly under the safety."

"Okay."

"So when you need to shoot, just move the safety down and squeeze the trigger."

"And that's it?"

"That's it."

She pulled the gun from her shoulder and thrust it back into his hands. "Thanks for the crash course, but I hope I'll never need it."

So did he. The grip was slick from the sweat on her palms. Her dislike of guns was genuine. It was a curious thing for a general's daughter, like her professed dislike of the army. "Why do you hate guns?" he asked.

"Where should I start? They're ugly." She wiped her hands on her jeans. "They smell like metal. They kill people. And they scare me."

"Why do they scare you?"

"What difference does it make?"

"I'd like to understand."

"For the good of our team? Morale of the troops?"

"You told me earlier that I don't know you," he said. He set the butt of the gun on the ground and leaned it against the tree beside him. "I think you're right. I'm trying to remedy that."

She looked away. Her right hand moved absently against her thigh, rubbing at a spot to the outside of her knee. At first it didn't appear as if she would answer him. Then she blew out a wobbly breath and spoke. "Did you ever see my father's gun collection?"

He remembered it vividly. The general had been exceedingly proud of the assortment of handguns he'd accumulated over the years. They'd included everything from a muzzle-loading relic of the Revolutionary War to a stainless steel Colt Anaconda. "Yes, I did. It was impressive."

"He kept it in a huge glass case that hung on the wall. No matter where we were posted, that case got moved with us. One of my earliest memories is my father lifting me up to show me the guns. He'd always be careful to keep the case locked when he wasn't around."

"That's good to hear."

"He knew how much damage they could inflict. He used to tell me exactly how dangerous they were. That's another one of my early memories."

"Do you think he overdid it?"

"Oh, no. He did the right thing. He taught me they weren't toys. I knew better than to touch them."

"So what happened?"

She crossed her arms and rubbed her palms over her jacket sleeves. The temperature had been dropping as the sun lowered, though it wasn't yet cold. Mitch suspected whatever chill she felt was from something else. "When I was around six," she said, "I came home from school and found that the case was open. My father was away, as he often was. My mother knew where he kept the key, because she was the one who had to deal with all the details of packing and unpacking whenever we moved. When I saw the case open, I thought we were moving again."

"Were you?"

"No." Her voice dropped. "My mother…had an accident."

"What kind of accident?"

"She was handling one of the guns and it went off."

"Was anyone hurt?"

"No. I helped her clean up so no one would know. After that, I didn't even want to look at a gun."

Mitch suspected there was more to the story. For one thing, the officer he'd known and admired wouldn't have kept loaded weapons in his display case. That just didn't fit. For another, he didn't think that having to sweep up some shattered china or crystal would have been enough to give Chantal such an aversion to weapons.

On the other hand, he was thinking of *this* Chantal, the one who had been proving her courage and resourcefulness all day. She'd kept her cool under fire. She had hiked for miles without complaint, even though she'd been hungry and her head had probably been killing her.

There had been plenty of changes in the last seventeen years. A lot of them were more subtle than the size of her breasts.

"It's ironic, isn't it?" she mused.

Yes, it *was* ironic. There had been a time when his main problem had been how to discourage her from chasing him. Now he was the one becoming preoccupied with her.

But he knew that wasn't what she was talking about. "What is?"

"That I hate guns, even though the Aerie's current client happens to head one of the country's largest arms manufacturers."

"Not really. You've made a success of this place, so you must be a practical woman. You wouldn't let your personal feelings interfere with your business."

"That's true. I wouldn't."

"The same way you're not letting your dislike of me stop us from working together."

"I don't dislike you, Mitch. I don't think I know you well enough."

He was surprised into a laugh. "Ouch."

A smile tugged at the corners of her mouth. "That didn't come out right. What I meant was that my memories of you were colored by what I wanted you to be. I couldn't see past my crush. Now that it's behind us, I'm not sure who you are."

"I was thinking the same thing about you." He picked up a lock of her hair and rubbed it between his fingers. "But if I mention any more of the changes I've noticed, you might get offended and start talking to me with your mother's perfect diction again and tell me to drop the subject."

Her budding smile dissolved. "Would I need to?"

He released her hair and lowered his hand. "No. I got the message the first time." He glanced past her to the lake. "It's dark enough. We'd better go while we can still see the path."

They walked the rest of the way in silence.

Chantal wasn't often in the boathouse after sunset. The space seemed functional and efficient when sunlight streamed through the big doors and the lake glistened in invitation, yet in the dark it seemed cavernous. Gloomy. The stars that shone beyond the windows were obliterated by the looming outlines of stored canoes. The smell of damp wood reminded her of dead fish. The *tsking* sound the water made as it lapped against the pilings was as nerve racking as a dripping tap.

A strange voice crackled behind her. "Everything's quiet on this side."

She jumped, an involuntary cry escaping her lips, before she realized the voice had come from the walkie-talkie on Mitch's belt.

"Didn't you hear that wolf?" another voice asked.

"That's a bird, Dodson."

"You sure?"

"Nothing to worry about. I'll meet you on the deck."

That was all. The voices were replaced by the faint hum of dead air.

Mitch squeezed her shoulder. "Are you okay?"

She nodded, but he probably couldn't see her well enough to make it out. "The walkie-talkie startled me."

"I want to leave it on until we're out of here."

Mitch had been switching the walkie-talkie off at regular periods during the day to conserve the battery. There hadn't been much to hear before. Now it sounded as if the men had organized patrols. At least two of them were out in the darkness somewhere.

But they had no reason to climb down to the lakeshore, she told herself. Those men wouldn't need a boat. They had a helicopter. They'd be patrolling around the main lodge, wouldn't they?

Mitch moved his hand beneath her hair and rubbed the back of her neck. "Relax," he said softly. "Another few minutes and we'll be out of here."

She closed her eyes to soak in his touch. When she opened them again, her vision had adjusted enough for her to make out more shapes in the gloom. "Wait where you are. I'll get a flashlight." She kept to the lighter wood of the walkway and made her way along it to the tall, rectangular storage cabinet in the corner.

Like everything else here, it wasn't locked. She opened the cabinet doors and felt around on the shelves until she grasped the long cylinder of a Maglight.

Mitch's cane thunked quietly as he followed. "Keep the beam down," he said.

She took his advice, holding the light close to her body to help shield it from the windows. She turned toward the center of the boathouse.

The space was empty, nothing but blackness where the thirty-foot-long expanse of gleaming mahogany should have been floating on the water.

Her brain couldn't process it at first. No. This wasn't possible. No one would have taken the launch on a tour today. No one could have. And the boat couldn't have drifted away by accident, because the doors were closed.

She started to tremble. There was only one explanation for the empty slip, but she didn't think she had the strength to absorb it. Not after what she'd already gone through. Not when the boat was her only chance of getting help to end this nightmare.

"Chantal," Mitch said. That was all. Just her name. Yet she could hear the regret in his voice. In her mind she heard the echo of how he'd sounded the last time he'd snuffed out her hopes.

She knelt on the edge of the walkway. The flashlight beam wobbled wildly around the interior before she managed to steady her grip and direct it downward.

The light reflected in flat, rainbow swirls. There was a film of oil on the surface of the water, and the scent of diesel fuel tainted the air. Chantal's stomach rolled. She leaned to the side to see past the oil slick.

The rocks at the lakeshore gave way to a fissured ledge that dropped off steeply here. The water beneath the boathouse was ten feet deep. The depth swallowed most of the light that wasn't reflected by the oil slick, yet some penetrated the blackness enough to throw back a glint of metal.

A narrow triangle took shape directly beneath her. It was the brass cap on the bow. It spread into curving sides. The shadows between them were spanned by wide, pale strips. Those would be the seats. The far end was lost in the darkness, but in her mind she could see the flag that had always fluttered from the stern.

The boat was here. It was on the bottom.

Mitch moved to stand beside her. He muttered a short, pungent oath. "We won't be going anywhere tonight."

The film of colors on the surface blurred. "They sank it."

"I should have anticipated this."

"But why?" She looked at him over her shoulder. "Why would they do this if they think we're dead?"

"So far, I've heard seven names mentioned over the air, which means Knox and his people could be outnumbered by the hostages. It would be smart to eliminate any potential transportation in case someone else managed to slip away. They probably would have done the same in the garage if I hadn't beat them to it."

Her gaze went past him to the canoes. They were ranged overturned along the wall in stacks of two, with the lowest one only a few feet off the floor and another one at shoulder height above it. Though she kept the beam of her light directed into the water, there was enough reflected illumination in the boathouse for her to notice what she hadn't before.

The sabotage hadn't been confined to the motorboat. Every canoe had at least one jagged hole in its hull. The canvas skins were shredded, the cedar strip ribs exposed like broken kindling. It looked as if someone had methodically taken an ax to each of them.

A sob came out of nowhere, ripping past her throat. She fought to keep the rest inside. She wasn't conscious of crossing the floor, yet somehow she stood in front of a ruined hull. Her fingers trembled as she traced the edges of a hole. Each craft had been lovingly fashioned by hand in the classic, voluptuous shape that was as much a pleasure to look at as to ride in. In total, they were almost as valuable as the seventy-year-old launch had been.

The financial loss would be significant. Though the resort was profitable, she didn't carry enough insurance to cover all of this. It would take years to replace what had likely taken only minutes to ruin. But it wasn't her balance sheet that made her feel like crying. It was the wanton destruction of something so beautiful.

The people they were up against had no qualms about killing. The events of this morning had proven that. The violence that had been done here had been cold-blooded and calculated. If the boathouse looked like this, what was happening at the Aerie?

Mitch cupped her elbow to turn her away from the canoes. "It'll be all right, Chantal."

There was so much confidence in his voice, she wanted to believe him. How she wished he really was the hero of her teenage fantasies.

He moved his thumb over her elbow. Even through her jacket she could feel the caress.

But neither of them was going to acknowledge it for what it was. She stepped back.

He dropped his hand.

She'd lost track of the number of times they'd acted out that same pattern today.

Suddenly, she found it frustrating. They had plenty of more important things to worry about than their personal history. She hated the way her thoughts kept returning to him, as if he were still the center of her world. She tapped the flashlight against her arm. "It's not all right. We can't swim all the way to Waterfalls."

"We've had another setback." He eased the flashlight from her grip and covered the head with his hand, dimming the light to a weak glow. "That just means we need to come up with another plan."

"A setback? You called my truck blowing up a setback, too. And I'd thought *I'd* had a problem with reality."

"You have every reason to be upset," he began.

"And of course, you don't get tired or hungry or scared

because you're a tough-as-nails Delta Force commando. It's not allowed."

"Chantal..."

"You're like any other army man. You don't have feelings unless they're assigned as part of your duties."

He stiffened. "There's no room for sentiment on a mission. That's how people get killed."

Her outburst made her feel petty. Again. Yet another pattern to frustrate her. She hugged her arms. "You were right. I'm upset, but I shouldn't take it out on you."

"Don't stop speaking your mind. I prefer your honesty to your über-polite mode."

"My what?"

"You know what I mean."

"Well, I don't have the energy left to be polite now. I don't know whether my friends are alive or dead. My home has been violated. My business is being destroyed before my eyes. We've wasted a day coming back here. I could have been halfway to the other end of the lake by now if you hadn't stopped me."

"Maybe. Or you could have had a dizzy spell, fallen down a cliff and broken your neck."

"My headache wasn't that bad."

"Yes, as it turned out your concussion appeared to be mild, but Knox has been thorough so far. We should consider the possibility that he might have gotten to your neighbors, too."

"I don't follow you."

"They're as isolated as you are, and just as vulnerable. We don't have any guarantee that we'd find help there."

"Are you saying there's nothing we can do?"

"Hardly. I told you before, Chantal, I don't give up."

"Then you have another plan?"

"I'm working on one. The first order of business is

finding a place to spend the night. We both need rest or we're not going to be any good to anyone. This place is too close to the main lodge. Do you have any other outbuildings?"

She tried to push her emotions aside and think rationally, the way he was. It wasn't easy to do when her feelings were as jumbled as they were now. "Besides the garage, only the woodshed, but that's even closer."

"Too risky."

"There were some housekeeping cabins in the next cove but we stopped using them when I took over the resort. They were too rough to fit into my vision for the place."

"I didn't see any cabins on the map in the lobby."

"No, they wouldn't be on it, but—"

"Quiet," he whispered, snapping off the flashlight. The boathouse was plunged into darkness. "Listen."

Men's voices drifted through the air. They were faint, yet in the absence of any other noise, it wasn't hard to distinguish the words.

"Don't know why we have to check it again. Knox's just being paranoid."

"Sure, Taddeo, but he pays good."

"Yeah. I think we should be getting a bigger share, seeing as how Benny's not pulling his weight."

"Huh, not a bad idea."

A pair of lights appeared beyond the window on the far side of the boathouse. They moved along the shore, as if following the path from the staircase.

Chantal's blood turned to ice. The voices weren't coming from the walkie-talkie this time. They were coming from outside.

Mitch gripped her arm and spun her toward the nearest canoe. "Get underneath," he whispered.

She had no problem obeying that order. Without giving

a thought to the layer of dust or the deck spiders that could be on the floor, she dropped to her stomach and slid into the hollow beneath the center of the overturned hull. An instant later, she felt Mitch's weight on her back.

He shifted to one side in order to switch off the walkie-talkie at his belt, then aligned his head with hers. His breath touched her ear. "Don't move."

She nodded. The voices were more distinct and approaching fast.

Mitch eased farther up her body. He brought his elbows beside her shoulders, laid the gun on the floor in front of her face and pointed the barrel toward the door. "No sound."

She nodded again.

"And if all hell breaks loose, roll into the water," he whispered, fitting his finger on the trigger. "I'll meet up with you where the trail curved to the lake."

There was no time to ask him what he meant by that or to tell him she had no intention of going anywhere without him. Before she could draw another breath, the door swung open and the big overhead lights were switched on.

Chapter 6

The boards beneath Chantal's cheek reverberated with heavy footsteps. Through the curving gap between the floor and the canoe gunwales, she could see two pairs of military-style boots. They were almost beside her. She couldn't see the men's faces. That meant the men couldn't see her, didn't it?

Or so she hoped. But her heart was beating so loudly, they must be able to hear it.

How big was the hole in the canoe's hull? She was facedown so she wouldn't be able see it without turning her head. What if the hole was right above them? What if the shadows weren't dark enough to hide them? What if the men could—

Mitch lifted one hand from the gun and squeezed her fingers.

Chantal clenched her jaw to keep her teeth from chattering.

"Nothing." It was the one who'd been called Taddeo. "Just like I thought."

One set of boots, the larger ones, moved past her. She followed them with her eyes as far as she could but didn't dare to move her head.

"What's in there?"

"Geez, Dodson, relax. It's just a bunch of boat stuff."

Chantal tensed. She felt Mitch do the same. They'd left the storage cupboard open.

But neither of the men remarked on it. There was a clatter as something fell to the floor. Paddles, by the sound of it. She started as an object thumped against the back of their hiding place. From the corner of her eye, she could see the flash of a red life jacket. Mitch returned his hand to the gun.

The man with the large boots came back. He picked up the life jacket. The canoe creaked, as if he was sitting against it. There was a rustle of cellophane and a metallic click. A lighter. A few seconds later, the smell of cigarette smoke wafted past her nose.

Dodson laughed. "So that's why you didn't complain about checking this place again."

"Those stairs are a bitch. Gotta have a rest before we start back up."

"Give me one of those, will you?"

Chantal didn't have a hope of calming her pulse. It was racing out of control. Instead she concentrated on breathing as silently as possible. It seemed the men had decided to take a smoke break. Here. Beside the very canoe she and Mitch were concealed beneath.

Mitch rested his cheek on the back of her head. Even through the layers of clothing that separated them, she could feel the increasing tension in his body. He was trying to keep most of his weight on his knees and elbows, but he was a large man. She was conscious of every inch of him. His chest pressed into her back with each breath he drew. That, and the cigarette smoke, made it hard for her to get enough air. She angled her face toward a gap in the floorboards, hoping for a fresh draft. She got a lungful of musty air tainted with diesel fumes instead.

"What are you going to do with your share of the take, Dodson? Get yourself another tattoo?"

He snorted. "I'm going to Vegas."

"Can't wait to lose it all again, huh?"

"No way. I've got a system. All I need is a stake." He shifted. The canoe creaked more loudly. "What you going to do with yours?"

"Figured I'd go down to South America. I heard they've got beaches where the chicks go topless."

"You better keep your cash in a nice, fat roll."

"Why?"

"So you can store it down your pants. That's the only way the babes'll notice you."

"That's crap. Babes love me. Didn't you see the way that chick up there couldn't stop looking at me?"

"Which one?"

"The little redhead. She reminds me of a stripper I knew in Chicago."

They were talking about Rhonda, her summer student. She was the only redhead among the hostages.

"Yeah, she's hot. We'll save her for the last."

"I don't care what Knox says, I say we do that kid first. He's getting on my nerves."

Do? she thought. What did they mean?

"Knox needs him to keep the mother in line."

There was a sucking sound as Taddeo drew hard on his cigarette. "I'll bleed the kid in front of them. That'll keep them all in line."

Realization dawned. Do. They'd meant kill. They were discussing killing Henry as casually as they'd spoken about spending their money. There had been no change in their tone. They continued to smoke and chat like a pair of ordinary workers on a coffee break. She pressed her lips tightly closed, fighting for control. Her chest spasmed.

Mitch took her hand again and squeezed. Hard. This time he didn't let go.

Dodson crushed his cigarette butt beneath his boot and stood. "Whatever. We can't start taking them out yet anyway, Taddeo. Knox said three more days. We gotta follow his plan."

"He's wasting our time, if you ask me. That fat dude ain't gonna screw with us." The canoe slid an inch backward as Taddeo pushed to his feet. His cigarette butt bounced on the floor and rolled toward Chantal's face. "He'll do what he's told."

She stared at the burning tip of the cigarette. Smoke curled from the dust around it. She thought about the wooden floorboards she and Mitch were lying on, the log walls around them and the oil slick the sunken launch had left on the water below. Would it ignite? She couldn't move. She was pinned beneath Mitch. She rubbed her head against his cheek, trying to draw his attention.

He bumped his chin on her temple. She couldn't tell whether he was acknowledging the problem or just cautioning her to keep still.

Mitch, she thought. *Look!*

The men started walking toward the door. "I still say we split Benny's share," Taddeo said.

"Sure. You tell him."

"We should get Bamford's too. All that college boy does is sit on his ass at the computer."

Mitch lifted his arm slowly and brought it down on

the cigarette, smothering the live tip under his leather sleeve.

Chantal exhaled in relief.

"This place gives me the creeps," Dodson said. "Sure wouldn't be my idea of a good time."

"Yeah. That water stinks."

"I thought you liked water."

"Nah, I like beaches. With naked chicks."

The lights went out. The door closed.

"Wait," Mitch whispered.

Keeping still was torture. Every nerve in her body was twitching. If she'd had a full stomach, she would have thrown up by now.

The men's conversation grew fainter as they walked away from the boathouse. Mitch remained motionless until the voices had faded completely, then he slid off her back, picked up his gun and rolled out from beneath the canoe.

She braced her forearms underneath her and lifted her chest, taking her first full breath in what seemed like hours. Despite the shot of oxygen, she felt light-headed.

"Are you okay?"

No, she was not okay. How could she be okay after what she'd heard?

He groped beneath the canoe until he touched her hip.

She jerked at the touch, which didn't make sense. He'd been plastered to her body for who knew how many minutes. Why was she suddenly sensitized to his touch?

Mitch skimmed his hand along her side to her shoulder. "Did I hurt you?"

"No. I..." She heard the quaver in her voice and swallowed hard. She tipped her head toward his hand.

Even though he'd nearly crushed her, she missed his weight. "Mitch, did you hear what they said?"

"Every word." He circled his fingers around her upper arm to tug her toward him. "Come on. We can't hang around. From the way those two were talking, they do regular patrols through here."

She crawled out, then sat back on her heels and slapped at the dust on her clothes. The cloud made her cough. She wiped her palms on her jeans. "They're going to kill Henry. They're going to kill all of them."

"That seems to be their plan."

"And I was about to cry over a bunch of boats. I thought things couldn't get worse, but they did."

He stretched his arm past her to retrieve the flashlight. He didn't turn it on. It wasn't necessary. The moon had risen and was shining through the south windows, spreading a silver glow throughout the boathouse. "We're still alive, Chantal." He looked around for the branch he'd been using as a cane. It was beside the pile of paddles that Taddeo had knocked over. Gripping it for balance, he shifted to kneel on his right knee. "That counts for a lot."

"What's wrong with those people? What do they want?"

"It sounded like they're after money."

"But—"

"It's got to be about Graham." He brushed at a pale streak of dust on the front of her jacket that she'd missed. "The Petherick Corporation has billions in assets. This must be an extortion attempt."

"We have to do something."

"We will."

She felt a jolt when his knuckles skimmed over her

breast. She caught his hand. To push him away? Or to prolong the contact? It was a little of both.

Mitch stilled. Or maybe it only seemed that way. A moment later he used the branch to lever himself to his feet, then drew her up to stand. "We know their timetable now. Three days."

"Before they start..." The words taunted her like snatches of a bad dream. "Before they start taking out the hostages."

"They wanted breathing room."

"For what?"

"They're waiting for something."

"I don't understand any of this."

"One of the men mentioned a computer. Could be they're using it to confirm a money transfer. Though if it was only money, it should take less than three days."

"I don't understand you, either," she said. She was still holding his hand, she discovered. She laced their fingers together. "How can you be so calm?"

"I'm not."

"Sure, you are. You're sorting through and analyzing what we heard as if you read it in an Intelligence file."

"We need every scrap of information we can get. It could prove valuable."

She had a wild urge to shake him. She stepped closer. "Don't you *feel*, Mitch?"

He looked at their joined hands. "You've mentioned that before."

"You act as if nothing touches you. Nothing bothers you. You're always in control."

He freed his fingers from hers, reversed his grip and held her palm to the side of his neck. "Don't mistake control for a lack of feeling, Chantal."

His pulse throbbed under her fingertips. It was racing almost as fast as hers.

"I feel everything," he said. "I'm as worried as you are about the welfare of the hostages, maybe more, because I've seen what can happen when situations like this go wrong. Same goes for what could have happened if Dodson and Taddeo had spotted us." He pressed her hand more firmly to his skin. "I'm concentrating on my duty so I can shut everything else out, but I can't turn it off entirely."

She shuddered. "That's what I mean. I can't turn it off, either."

"And if things weren't already complicated enough, for the last ten minutes, I've felt your body under mine and your hair tickling my cheek. A minute ago I felt the curve of your breast under your jacket and right now I can feel the trembling in your fingers. I've been doing my damnedest to ignore all of that, too."

Leave it to Mitch not to beat around the bush. He'd brought up what she hadn't wanted to face. She'd been aware of everything he'd said, and then some.

It didn't seem right, with life and death in the balance, to give any thought to her physical needs, yet it wasn't only worry that was making her heart pound. It was plain, old-fashioned chemistry. She splayed her hand within his grasp. Her thumb traced the edge of his jaw. The day's growth of his beard stubble bristled. The skin beneath was warm and taut as only a man's could be.

"The adrenaline's making us jumpy," he said. "It's a natural reaction to what happened here. Now that the danger's passed, your body's looking for an outlet for the extra energy."

Tingles continued to chase across her nerves where she touched him. Yes, it was likely adrenaline that was causing her heightened sensitivity. She'd told herself the same thing this morning.

The trouble was, it didn't make the sensations any less real.

In the moonlight, Mitch's features looked harsh, devoid of color. There was no softness to the shadows under his eyebrows and cheekbones, no gradual shading of the sharp angles of his nose and chin. The grooves beside his mouth appeared chiseled into stone.

And yet his pulse continued to accelerate, just like hers. And his eyes, oh, they sparkled with that special warrior's gleam. She'd have to be dead to ignore that. The fear Chantal had felt only moments ago flipped into another emotion entirely. She swayed against him, seized by a primitive desire for contact.

"Chantal..."

She heard his caution and didn't care. She wrapped her arms around his waist, fitting their bodies together so that there was no space left between. Her back still bore traces of his warmth. Now she welcomed that warmth into her arms, her breasts and her thighs.

He cupped his hand over her shoulder to ease her away.

Chantal shrugged off his grasp and nuzzled her face past his jacket collar. She kissed his neck.

She discovered that Mitch's skin tasted the same as she remembered. Soap. Sunshine. The tang like warm cotton that was uniquely his.

A tremor went through his frame. Heat seemed to pour off him in waves. He rested his hand on her back, no longer trying to push her away, yet not pulling her closer, either. He held himself rigid. Restrained. "You're strung out. You'll feel better once you sleep."

She rubbed her nose against the angle of his jaw. He

smelled like leather and dust. The last time she'd held him, he'd smelled like rain. She lifted on her toes to bring her mouth to his. She spoke against his lips. "It isn't sleep that I need."

"Trust me." His voice was hoarse. "You don't want to do this."

The present merged with the past. In her mind, she heard the echo of Mitch's voice. *Chantal, stop. You're not thinking straight. You don't want to do this.*

He was right. Both times. But once again, she shut out the voice of reason. She followed her instincts and kissed him.

The contact was electrifying. She remembered the touch of his mouth as vividly as she remembered the taste of his skin. Why was that? She'd kissed him only once before. It had been brief and awkward—she'd been straining toward him while he'd been backing away. She'd done her best to block the memory of that particular humiliation, yet her subconscious must have stored it all these years because he didn't feel like a stranger. He felt familiar. No, more than familiar, *right.* His mouth settled over hers as perfectly as their bodies were fitting together.

And this time, he wasn't pushing her away. He flattened his hand at the small of her back and hauled her against him. Then he tilted his head and slid his tongue into her mouth.

The pleasure of that joining astonished her. It traveled to every intimate place in her body. She arched into him, tunneling her fingers into his hair to hold him exactly where he was. She wouldn't lose him again. She didn't want this to end.

To her delight, he wasn't trying to go anywhere. A moan rumbled from his chest. He withdrew his tongue, only to plunge it in harder and faster. He took full possession of her mouth, as if he had every right, as if they'd both been waiting for this moment. The world contracted around them. All she was aware of was his taste, his strength, the slick moisture on her lips, the hot breath on her cheek.

Any remaining echoes of the past were overpowered by the sheer carnality of the kiss. This was no awkward encounter between a teenager and her fantasy hero. This was frank, sexual passion.

Chantal shuddered as the rhythm of the kiss resounded between her legs. Never had she felt such an imperative… *need*. Her body was pulsing. Without being conscious of making a decision, she hooked one foot behind his calf and angled her hips to his. She showed him what she wanted, oblivious to everything except the desire to get closer.

Mitch lost his balance and staggered backward, breaking off the kiss. He released his hold on her, stumbled into the heap of paddles and fell with a crash that seemed to echo past the boathouse walls and across the lake.

The abrupt loss of contact was a shock. Her chest heaved as she struggled to understand what had happened. She toed aside the paddles and extended her hand to Mitch.

He wordlessly waved away her help. He sat up on his own, looking as shaken as she felt. He raked his fingers through his hair and swore.

So help her, despite where they were, despite the noise they'd just made, she wanted to drop to the floor beside him and continue what they'd started. Her body was thrumming with a mindless need for completion. "Are you all right?" she asked.

He snorted a laugh that held no humor. "Sure. Great. What about you?"

She wasn't sure *how* she was. She wasn't sure of anything.

Except that she wished they hadn't stopped. "I'm sorry, Mitch. I wasn't thinking."

He found his cane among the paddles and stood. He stared at her for a long minute, then swore again and turned for the door. "Yeah. That makes two of us."

Chapter 7

The cabin was slowly being reclaimed by the forest. Brush obscured the front entrance. An uprooted tree had fallen across the slope behind it in a way that left one large limb half covering the roof. Mitch didn't believe it would be visible from the air, and the overgrown path that led to it was no more noticeable than a game trail. The interior was in surprisingly good shape, with one all-purpose main room and a small bedroom at the back. Much of the original furniture remained, and the structure's solid construction had kept animal damage to a minimum.

It was the ideal spot to hole up in. Despite the fact that there was only one bed.

But that was a minor issue, Mitch reminded himself. He had to concentrate on survival, both his and Chantal's. They were the only hope for the hostages. There was no room for personal feelings.

Right. Sure. He could tell himself that as many times as he wanted, but his body wasn't listening.

Mitch sat up, flexing his shoulders to work out the stiffness. He'd spent the night on the floor in front of a cold wood stove on a pallet of boat cushions that he'd scavenged from the boathouse. He'd figured he wouldn't get any sleep if he shared the bed with Chantal.

As it turned out, he hadn't slept much anyway. For most of the night he'd been thinking about what it would have been like if he *had* shared her bed.

He drew up one knee, rested his arm on it and turned to look past the small wooden table and chairs to the bedroom doorway. Sunrise wasn't far off, although the light that filtered through the front window was dim. Clouds had rolled in during the night, which was lucky since the overcast had kept the temperature from dropping as much as it might have. Chantal was lying curled on her side, her arms clutching a fold of the quilt they'd found in a trunk at the foot of the bed. It stank of mothballs, but she hadn't complained. She'd barely spoken to him after they'd left the boathouse.

He couldn't blame her.

What the hell had come over him? He'd known better. She'd been upset. She'd needed comfort. He'd blown it as thoroughly as he had the last time she'd kissed him.

Only this time, he hadn't run. For one thing, he wasn't capable of running. For another, he...

What? He wanted her? That was no excuse. He normally had no trouble controlling his impulses. Regardless of how good Chantal smelled, or how luscious her curves had felt against his body, he should have restrained himself. Where was his conscience?

Nowhere, apparently. The problem was, after spending a full day with the new Chantal, the old taboos that had kept him from regarding her as a desirable woman no longer applied. The ten-year gap in their ages didn't seem relevant now that she was thirty-five. He didn't report to her father. They weren't living in the gossip mill of a military base. He had nothing to weigh on his conscience.

Except the lives of fourteen innocent people, including Chantal.

Mitch rubbed his eyes, then dropped his forehead against his palm. He was going in circles. He'd faced the fact that he was attracted to this woman. That wasn't going to change simply because he found it inconvenient. He had to try harder to deal with it.

You're an army man. You don't have feelings unless they're assigned as part of your duties.

She'd come uncomfortably close to the mark with that comment. He hadn't always been that way, though. When he'd started out, every day had been a gift. He'd done his duty because he'd loved it, not because it was the only thing he had left in his life. Being a soldier was in his blood. Chantal had told him that she hated the army. Mitch had known military service was his destiny from the time he'd been old enough to understand what it was his dad did. Like Chantal, he'd been raised as an army brat, only his father had been a staff sergeant, not a general.

Mitch had been the first Redinger to become an officer. His family had been exceedingly proud of the accomplishment. So had Mitch. His life had seemed to be unfolding precisely as he'd planned. It was true, as Chantal had said, that he'd had career ambitions. There was nothing wrong with that. He'd been determined to prove his worth not only to the army but to his family and to himself.

At first, that crush of hers had been merely embarrassing, since she'd had a way of showing up wherever he was.

He'd tried to regard her as a little sister and had striven for patience, but she'd misinterpreted his kindness as encouragement. As her pursuit had become more open, rumors had begun to circulate that he was sleeping with General Leduc's daughter in order to gain her influence with her father.

As with any rumor, denial only fueled the speculation. It had been next to impossible to fight the sidelong glances and the barely veiled innuendos. He'd begun to lose the respect of the other officers. The same thing had been happening with the enlisted men: more than a few had approached the line of insubordination. Although the general had given him the benefit of the doubt, there had been a creeping strain in their relationship as well. If things had continued the way they'd been headed, Mitch would likely have ended up sidelined to some radar base in Alaska.

That final night, when Chantal had coaxed him to the Leduc house and had refused to take no for an answer, Mitch had run out of patience. He'd been less concerned about her feelings than the disastrous consequences of being discovered in such a compromising position. Afterward, he'd put an end to the problem by requesting a transfer himself.

The decision had changed his life. It had led him to enter the Special Forces. He'd embarked on a career path that suited him to a tee. He hadn't contacted Chantal again because he'd convinced himself that making a clean break was the kindest thing he could have done for her.

He wasn't proud of the way he'd put his ambition first. Nor was he proud of how very much he'd been tempted to take Chantal up on her offer.

Was that why he hadn't been able to stop himself from

kissing her yesterday? Because there was unfinished business between them?

Or because she was challenging his ability to feel?

He looked at his hand. He was rubbing his wedding band with the tip of his thumb, something he often found himself doing without thinking.

At times the ability *not* to feel was vital to a man's survival. Focusing on his duty always helped.

His men regarded him as hard at times. That's what a good commander had to be. He couldn't show any weakness or indecision, not if he was to maintain discipline. For the same reason, as an officer he couldn't join in the camaraderie the enlisted men enjoyed. Being able to channel his emotions into his job was an asset in his line of work.

It had taken years of dedication to mold Eagle Squadron into the elite force it was now. The team members were as tight as brothers, as loyal as any family. They would be willing to die for each other as readily as they would be willing to kill. As he'd told Chantal, a team couldn't function at its best if tension existed among the members.

The history between him and Chantal presented enough of a problem. What had happened yesterday took the tension to a whole different level.

Something scraped against the cabin's front window. Mitch automatically reached for his gun before he realized the noise had been made by a twig brushing over the glass. A breeze had come up. The light was strengthening. He could see the shadow of Chantal's lashes on her cheeks. Her lips were parted and lax against a corner of the quilt that she'd tucked beneath her chin. Watching her as she slept, it was hard to believe the heat of their kiss. How could a mouth that soft have drawn him in so tightly? How could such a sweet-looking face have inspired the passion that had broken through his restraint?

He returned his gaze to his ring. It would be seven years this December since Dianne had died. He hadn't had any desire to commit to another woman since then, though he did have the sexual needs of a normal, healthy male. He hadn't lived like a monk for the last seven years, yet he'd never experienced the overwhelming lust that Chantal had triggered. He'd known the location wasn't secure, he'd seen she'd been overwrought, and yet he'd been making love to her mouth. If he hadn't tripped over those paddles, he was sure in another few seconds they would have been doing the real thing.

So what would happen if he walked to the bedroom, lay down beside her and used another one of those kisses to wake her up?

He rose to his feet. He stood where he was for a full minute before he managed to make himself turn to the door and leave the cabin.

This morning, at least, duty won.

Chantal's molars watered as she looked at the skewered trout. She broke off a piece and rammed it in her mouth. The delicate flavor burst over her tongue like a symphony, but she was too ravenous to take the time to savor it as it deserved. She swallowed fast and took another piece. Nothing that Walter had been able to whip up in the Aerie's kitchen with all its state-of-the-art gadgets could come close to this taste. "This is delicious," she mumbled, not wanting to stop chewing long enough to empty her mouth. "How on earth did you manage it?"

Her mother would have been appalled at her lack of manners, but it felt glorious to eat something substantial again. She hadn't realized how hungry she'd been.

She could feel her energy return with each morsel she swallowed.

She and Mitch were sitting on a piece of driftwood a few yards from the lakeshore. The boughs of a birch tree cut the wind to a light breeze. The Aerie and its long dock weren't visible from this cove, so Mitch had decided there was little risk of being spotted if they ate outside. Though the cloud cover thickened, the rain it promised held off for now. The air was pleasantly crisp and for the first time in over twenty-four hours, she was feeling more like herself. Mitch had been right. She'd needed rest. She'd also really, *really* needed food.

He had already finished his fish down to the bones. He flicked what was left into the water and used the empty skewer to point downward. A shallow, metal tin rested on the rounded pebbles at his feet. "That's what's left of a kerosene lantern that I found in the cabin. I made it into a mini camp stove. The advantage of using that is the kerosene burns clean. Firewood would have smoked."

"Is that what they teach you in the Special Forces?"

"No, I think I saw it on *MacGyver.*"

Her cheeks puffed out with a laugh. She swallowed fast, not wanting to lose a speck of the trout. "How did you get the fish?"

"I took some fishing gear from the supply cupboard in the boathouse."

Her smile faded. "You went back on your own? When?"

"Just before dawn. You were still sleeping."

"You should have woken me up."

"You were safer where you were. The cabin's not on the lodge's map, and it can't be seen from the air."

She cleaned the last of the meat from her fish, got rid

of the bones, then sucked the juice from her fingers. "I could have helped you."

He looked at her mouth. "I managed to find a number of useful items. Matches. Rope. A fish-cleaning knife."

She could feel his gaze as if he'd touched her. He'd been careful not to, though. He'd made sure there was plenty of space between them on the driftwood log, just as he'd made sure to knock on the cabin door before he'd invited her outside for breakfast.

She was grateful for his matter-of-fact approach to their sleeping arrangements and to the necessities that arose while living together. He wasn't making a big deal out of keeping his distance from her—he was simply doing it. Obviously, he wanted to avoid a repeat of what had happened yesterday evening. Of course, so did she. That was the only sensible course of action. She still couldn't believe what had come over her. She stopped licking her fingers and lowered her hand to her lap. "Thanks for the meal."

"My pleasure. I've put out a few baited lines. As long as you can stomach the idea of more fish, that'll be our lunch, too."

"It sounds great."

"I found a spring behind the cabin. How's the water quality around here?"

"Excellent. We pump our water from the lake. We run it through a reverse osmosis filter before we supply it to the guests, just to be sure there are no contaminants, but the water from the spring should be as safe to drink as it is."

"Good. In that case, here." He handed her a clear plastic bottle filled with water. "I found the bottle in the boathouse, too. I cleaned it out and filled it from the spring."

"Thanks."

"You can keep it with you. Make sure you stay hydrated."

She marveled at how efficiently he was seeing to their physical needs. She took days to plan a menu and obtain supplies for a party of guests. "You've really been busy."

"Just taking care of priorities. How's your head this morning?"

She paused to consider his question. The headache that had dogged her yesterday had reduced to a distant throb. She hadn't noticed the absence of pain until he'd asked. "Much better," she said. "How's your ankle?"

"The swelling's worse, but that's to be expected. The pain's not as bad." He held up his cane. "I should be able to get rid of this branch before long."

"That should make things easier for you."

He nodded. "Now that we're more or less healthy, I have an idea about how we can contact help."

She leaned forward fast. "Oh, Mitch. How?"

"There should be a radio in their helicopter. We'll use it."

She couldn't believe she'd heard him correctly. "You've heard the names of at least seven men. There could be more, and they'd all be armed."

"And there are two of us. I've planned missions where the odds are a lot worse than that. Hear me out."

She gestured for him to continue.

He leaned down to move his improvised camp stove to one side, then cleared away the stones. Once he'd bared an area of sand, he smoothed it flat with his hand. "This is the main building," he said, drawing a rectangle in the sand with the stick he'd used to cook his trout. He drew another, smaller rectangle and then a circle. "Here's the garage, and here's the landing spot on the top of the hill. Show me all the trails that go between them."

She slid off the log and knelt in front of his diagram. She used her own stick to draw in the lines, taking her time to make sure she was right. "The main trail is bordered with rocks," she said, drawing a double line. "There's another one that comes up from the west side of the hill," she added.

"Where do the trees stop?"

"Below the crest." She sketched a flattened square around the landing circle to show the extent of the trees. "There's no place to hide on that rock. We cleared everything away to make it safe for a helicopter to land. Anyone could see you."

"Which means I'll be able to see them, too."

"Are you going to wait until dark?"

"It would be better for the hostages if I don't. The sooner we can contact the authorities and get a rescue initiated, the better."

"Are Knox's men still patrolling around the Aerie?"

"From what I've overheard, they are. It makes me think he could be former military."

"Because of his thoroughness?"

"Yes. Most civilians would assume the area was secure because of its isolation, but he's not taking chances. He's established a perimeter and is posting watches."

"If he's from the military," she said slowly, "that could be how he knew about Graham. The Petherick Corporation wouldn't be well known in civilian circles."

"Good point. And if Knox has had military training, he's going to want to maintain discipline and stick to his schedule, no matter what. I figure I'll have a window of at least ten minutes as his men do their rounds. I can approach from here," he said, pointing to the trail on the west. He then indicated a spot at the edge of the tree line. "You can be positioned here where I'll be able to see you but anyone coming from the lodge can't. You can signal me if there's trouble."

"How?"

"You can use the flashlight we got from the boathouse. This cloud cover looks as if it's going to get thicker. I'll notice the beam if you direct it straight at me."

She looked at the rectangle that represented her home. Her sanctuary. Part of her still couldn't believe this was real. Waves lapped against the pebbles on the shore, sounding just the same as they had on countless other mornings. Birch leaves rustled in the wind overhead. The delicate taste of fresh trout lingered in her mouth. How could she be sitting here, calmly planning what was beginning to resemble a military operation?

Then her mind filled with images of what she'd seen through the Aerie's front window yesterday morning, and reality descended with a thud.

It had been more than a day since those men had arrived. Were her friends still unharmed? Had they eaten or slept? Were they being mistreated? What would happen when their three days were up?

As if he'd followed the direction of her thoughts, Mitch touched her arm.

She jerked at the contact. Her hand obliterated half the sketch. She smoothed out what she could and started to redraw it. "Sorry," she mumbled.

"You won't need to do anything except be my lookout."

"I'll do whatever I have to. It's my home. The people there are my responsibility."

"I won't knowingly put you in danger."

"We're a team, Mitch."

"Right." He took the stick from her hand. He was careful not to touch her this time. "And because we are, before we get started there's something we need to talk about."

She brushed off her hands and resumed her seat on the driftwood log. "What?"

"Our kiss."

She should have known he wouldn't let it slide. When had he ever hesitated to speak his mind? "There's really nothing to discuss. It was a mistake."

"Yes, it was. It was reckless and irresponsible. I have no excuse. I apologize."

It would be easy to allow him to assume the blame. He appeared to want to. He'd always had a noble streak. "I started it, Mitch. You did your best to discourage me. I'm the one who should apologize."

"If it makes you feel better, go ahead, but you couldn't have been expected to understand what was happening."

"You mean the adrenaline."

"Yes."

"So it's happened to you before?"

"I've experienced an adrenaline rush during a hazardous situation on a mission, yes."

"And have you channeled that rush into a kiss?"

His eyebrows shot upward. "Hell, no."

He seemed so dumbstruck, she was surprised into a smile. "Sorry. I wasn't questioning your…uh… preferences…" She closed her mouth before she could say more. Considering his enthusiastically heterosexual response to their kiss, casting any doubt on his sexual orientation would be ludicrous.

He appeared to think so as well. He blew out his breath on a low chuckle. "Right. I walked straight into that one.

The fact is, we seldom have females present during a mission."

"I suppose not."

"Although on a few of the occasions when we have, it's led to similar problems. Not with me, of course, but I've had to caution some of my men to maintain their objectivity."

"Really?"

"Even tough-as-nails Delta Force commandos have human urges."

He'd used her own words. She made a face. "Do you remember *everything* I said?"

"It's important to me. I'm trying to get to know you."

"For the good of our army of two."

"Yes."

"Well, I assure you that I'm not in the habit of forcing kisses on unwilling men. You just seem to have a way of bringing that out in me."

"In case you hadn't noticed, I wasn't unwilling."

"No, not this time anyway."

"Chantal—"

"Please," she said, holding up her hand. "Don't explain again. We covered that yesterday. I do understand why you walked out the last time. It was the only honorable thing you could have done."

"You were too young. And I was concerned about my career."

"Yes. Really, I do understand. I only brought that up because I don't want you to think I'm trying to relive the past or anything like that. As a rule, I'm fully in control of my impulses these days."

"I noticed you've changed. You're more reserved."

"I've learned to be."

"Is that because of me?"

For once, a sharp retort didn't come to her lips. Maybe it was the grilled fish. Or maybe she was finally putting her issues with him into perspective. She shook her head. "Only partly. I latched onto you because I was searching for someone to take me away from a life I didn't know how to change. I saw you as my fantasy hero. I gave you capabilities that no man really has."

"Why did you want to change your life?"

She hedged. Her new comfort with him didn't extend that far. "What teenager doesn't? I had to learn that I needed to rely on myself, no one else. I had to take charge of my own life."

"Is that why you came to the Aerie?"

"I have everything I need here. I love my job. I love this place. My staff are like my family. Most of my clients become friends."

"It's a drastic change from how you used to live."

"Not entirely. Don't you remember how much entertaining my mother used to do? I learned how to be a good host and how to take care of guests from the time I was a child."

"Okay, I can see that."

"But you're right about one thing. The Aerie itself is the complete opposite of a military base. It's beautiful and peaceful. Out here, the troubles of the rest of the world don't seem to matter. There's no rank to keep in mind, no protocol to worry about and few schedules to keep. For six months of the year, I'm able to live in a place where I feel totally free."

"Six months," he repeated. "Where do you live in the winter?"

"I have a small apartment in Bethel Corners. It's a lovely little town, but can't compare to living on the lake."

"Doesn't the isolation bother you?"

"No, it's invigorating. Look around you," she said, sweeping her hand in a wide arc. "There's more power in the natural world than in any amount of man-made constructs. This hill and this lake will be here long after all the army bases I grew up on are nothing but ruins and no one remembers why all the wars were fought."

A hawk cried overhead. Mitch tilted his head back to follow its flight for a while before he spoke again. "How come you ended up hating the army, Chantal?"

Once again, he had managed to zero in on a thread she wasn't comfortable pursuing. "It was probably the guns."

"Sure."

"How did we get onto this topic, anyway?"

He shifted to sit sideways, leaving his left leg stretched out and drawing his right foot onto the log. He rested his forearms on his up-drawn knee and leaned toward her. "We were talking about our kiss."

"Oh."

"You said you only kiss willing men."

"As opposed to throwing myself at men who run away."

"There must be a lot of the first kind."

"What does that mean?"

"Willing men. Men who would consider themselves lucky to be kissed by you. I can't imagine there being a shortage."

"Is that a convoluted way of paying me a compliment?"

"It depends. If you're going to get prickly about it, then no. That was actually a convoluted way of asking you about your personal life."

She frowned. "I don't see that it's relevant to our continued functioning as a team."

"It's not. I'm just curious."

"I'm not currently seeing anyone special."

"Why not?"

"For one thing, I'm far too busy. During the season we're usually booked solid. Running the Aerie is a long-term commitment. For another, I like my life the way it is. I'm not interested in having a relationship."

"Neither am I," he said. "Everything you just said goes for me, as well. My work is too demanding to leave much time for a personal life, and that suits me fine. I don't have any desire for a serious relationship."

"Then we have something in common."

"Uh-huh. But we also have a problem."

"What?"

"It's broad daylight, and we're not particularly stressed or in imminent danger, so there's no adrenaline in play here, but I still want to kiss you."

His declaration triggered another round of triumphant arm pumps from the girl deep inside Chantal. She turned her head aside, unwilling to let him see the pleasure that surely must show in her eyes.

She'd just told him that she didn't want to relive the past. And she didn't. She never again wanted to be that needy girl who loved him. The mere thought of being that vulnerable brought on a quick jab of panic.

Yet that wasn't what was happening between them, was it? Nor was it what she felt. It was one good aspect that had come from their kiss in the boathouse. She could never confuse the lust it had aroused with the sweet, pure love that had once filled her heart. Yesterday's kiss had been about sex, plain and simple. It had been entirely physical.

"We're both adults, Mitch," she said. "We should be able to control our hormones."

"We. Is that your way of saying you're attracted to me?"

The question was ludicrous. How could a woman not be attracted by the way he looked this morning, with the tangled forest as a backdrop and the churning sky overhead?

His cheeks were darkened with a day's growth of beard in a way that accentuated the dramatic lines of his face, yet his tousled hair looked appealingly boyish. He'd discarded his jacket, and the loose neckline of his sweatshirt had pulled to one side, revealing the strong ridge of his collarbone. His sleeves were pushed up to his elbows, showing off forearms that were contoured with ropy muscle beneath a dusting of soft, black hair. His pants were stretched in tight folds of cotton that fingered across his thigh like a caress. He'd left his gun leaning on the log behind him, and his improvised stove rested at his feet.

Not only was he a rugged, drop-dead-sexy specimen of manhood, he also cooked.

Chantal had a mad desire to laugh. "To be honest, Mitch, you're the last man in the world who I would want to be attracted to."

"You're ducking the question."

"Did anyone ever tell you that you can be too direct at times?"

"In my line of work, it's an asset."

"I can imagine."

"And you're still ducking the question."

"Fine. Yes, I find you attractive, but that shouldn't interfere with our ability to work together any more than our history did."

He pulled his foot off the log and stood. "I know. We have bigger priorities."

"Too many people are depending on us."

"Absolutely. I've thought the same thing myself."

"Not to mention the fact that neither of us is interested in any kind of relationship."

"That's true." He regarded her steadily. "And even if you were, I'm the last man in the world you'd want one with."

"Exactly."

He nodded. "Swell. I'm glad we cleared that up."

Chapter 8

The clouds scudded low and fast, coming in from the northeast in dark-bellied banks of gray. Chantal could see the blurred outline of a squall as it worked its way across the lake, driving rows of whitecaps in front. So far, the rain hadn't reached the crest of the hill, but it would be here before long. She could taste the moisture in the air. She curled one arm around the pine she stood beside and continued her scrutiny of the cleared rock.

The black helicopter sat in the center of the painted landing circle, as ominous-looking as the clouds. Its massive main propeller vibrated in the wind, giving off a low-pitched drone. No bright paint or corporate logo relieved the dull finish of the fuselage. According to Mitch, it was an old Huey, which had once been the workhorse of the army. Judging by the gun mounts beneath the nose, he speculated it could have originally been used by the military and sold off as surplus equipment. He'd been pleased about that, since he was familiar with this model.

For what had to be the tenth time in the last two minutes, she tried to peer through the glass windows into the cockpit, but all she could see was the reflection of the rain clouds.

"Mitch, hurry," she whispered.

During their slow climb up the hill, he'd explained to her how he would send a message. He didn't need to start up the engine. He planned to use the aircraft's massive batteries to power up the instrument panel and the radio, then tune to the emergency broadcast frequency. He'd made it sound simple.

As simple as remaining undetected while they looked through the Aerie's front window yesterday morning? Or as simple as escaping in her truck afterward? Or taking out her boat last night?

Mitch, please, hurry up and finish!

She returned her attention to the path that led down to the Aerie. She and Mitch had waited through two complete rotations of Knox's patrol schedule to be sure they had it right. If the men followed the same pattern, no one would be due to appear for another ten minutes at least. That would give Mitch plenty of time. Unless someone decided to come earlier to beat the rain.

As if her thoughts had made it happen, a handful of drops splatted on the rock beyond the trees.

Chantal pressed closer to the pine as the squall finally arrived. Her jacket kept her upper half dry, but rain drilled against her jeans and her hair. Within minutes, water trickled down the back of her neck and her legs were numb. But no matter how wet she got, she couldn't move. Mitch would be trusting her to be his eyes. He said he would be looking here for her signal. Her warning could save his life.

Yes, he trusted her. He no longer thought of her as an overindulged, impulsive child. They were beginning to function as a team, in spite of their past and the chemistry they'd acknowledged between them. The magnitude of that fact wasn't lost on her, yet there was no imaginary celebration from her inner teenager this time. The stakes were too high.

She wiped the rain from her eyes and dropped her hand to her leg as she did another slow scan of the hilltop. It had rained the night Mitch had left, too. It had rained for the entire week after her mother's funeral. Chantal had gone to the cemetery every day. She had stood for hours beside the fresh mound while the rain dripped from her black umbrella. Sometimes a gust of wind would drive the raindrops against her legs and soak her skirt—her mother had never liked her wearing jeans, it wasn't ladylike. Mostly, though, the rain had pattered straight down, as if the sky was too exhausted to spend any extra energy on the task.

She remembered that detail about the weather, because she'd felt the same way. She'd wept, but her tears had seeped from her eyes gently, like the rain. To her mother's friends, the other officers' wives, she'd appeared the dedicated, grieving daughter. They'd all seen how close the pair of them had been. From the time Chantal had been six years old and had come home to find her mother with her father's pearl-handled Webley in her hand, she'd been Bernadette Leduc's shadow. And Bernadette had become the center of her daughter's existence.

The general hadn't gone with her on those graveside vigils. He'd grieved for his wife in his own way, a manly dignified-officer way, with a bottle of bourbon behind the closed door of his study. He'd been uncomfortable with her displays of emotion because they had reminded him too much of Bernadette's. His withdrawal had frustrated her. Like their friends, he'd never understood the complex relationship between his wife and his daughter.

No one did, because she'd never told a soul. So they hadn't guessed how much anger had been mixed with her grief, and how much resentment she'd felt over having a childhood that no child should have gone through. After a week of standing in wet shoes on the soggy grass, searching for a way to fill the void of her sudden freedom, something inside Chantal had finally snapped. She hadn't wanted to be alone. She hadn't wanted to be the strong one anymore. She'd wanted someone to take care of *her* for a change. Above all, she'd wanted to be loved.

So she'd turned to Mitch. She'd laid her heart bare. When he hadn't wanted it, she'd bared her body, too.

The memory of that night still stung, even after their oh-so-adult conversation this morning and all the rationalizing she'd done since then.

Regardless of the pain, it was probably a good thing that the memories were being purged. She'd carried them around for almost half her life, along with her resentment. That couldn't have been healthy. It was high time to let them go, wasn't it? Let them heal. She and Mitch were different people now. That's what she'd told him yesterday morning on the dock.

God, had it only been yesterday? It felt as if she'd lived another lifetime in one day. She wiped the rain from her face, then used her hand to shield her eyes from the downpour.

Someone was coming up the path from the lodge. A green, hooded rain poncho covered the figure from his head to his knees. It looked like one of the Aerie's ponchos. They had a supply of foul-weather gear for guests who got caught without their own. Tommy and Rhonda had been making use of them during the rainy weather last month. The figure was Tommy's height, and he moved with the springy step that was characteristic of the young student. Was it possible that he had slipped away?

For a moment, wild hope superseded logic and Chantal opened her mouth to call to him. But then a gust of wind flattened the poncho across his chest. She saw the outline of a gun that was held beneath the rubberized vinyl.

She fumbled inside her jacket for the flashlight, pointed it directly at the windshield of the helicopter and switched it on. She counted two seconds, turned it off for two seconds, then repeated the sequence twice more.

The rain was coming down like a curtain. What if Mitch couldn't see her signal? She tried again, all the while making sure to keep the tree trunk between her and the approaching man. He was almost beside her now. He was making no effort to walk silently. She could hear his scuffing footsteps over the sound of the wind.

She clicked off the light and lowered it to her side. Her elbow caught the strap of the gun that hung from her shoulder. It started to slide. She grabbed it fast to keep it from falling to the ground. The metal clip that held the strap to the stock clinked.

Damn! She hadn't wanted to keep this gun. She had good reasons to hate guns. It was completely useless to her. But Mitch had insisted. He hadn't wanted to leave her defenseless. She'd had to go along with him because otherwise, he wouldn't have agreed to her acting as his lookout in the first place.

The man in the poncho paused, as if he'd heard the noise. He gave a cursory glance around the area, then started forward once more. He was heading straight for the helicopter.

Chantal thought she saw movement inside the cockpit. She got as close to the edge of the trees as she dared and used her light again, hoping against hope that Mitch could see the warning. He might not be able to see the man. The green poncho would blend into the pines.

The man in the poncho must have seen the movement in the cockpit, too. He cupped his hands over his mouth. "Hey, Molitor!" he yelled. "That you?"

The spot where the helicopter rested was the highest point on the rock hilltop. Because of that, Chantal could see beneath it from where she stood. Between the bottom of the fuselage and the landing struts, she watched as Mitch jumped to the ground.

"Since you're out there, you finish this circuit!" the man shouted. He stopped and did a sudden about-face. "I didn't sign on for this scut work," he muttered. His eyes widened. "Hey! Who the hell are you?"

He'd turned so quickly, she hadn't had a chance to douse her light. He was staring right at her. He wasn't wearing a ski mask, so she had a clear view of his face. He appeared as shocked as she was, but it didn't last. He flipped back his poncho and swung his gun in her direction.

Chantal acted without thinking. She hurled her flashlight at him. The cylinder spun through the rain in a blur of chrome and glass. It struck him squarely on his nose.

He slapped one hand to his face as he staggered back a step. Blood oozed between his fingers. "You bitch!" He returned his hand to his gun. More blood spurted from a horizontal gash on his nose. "You're gonna pay for that! Drop your gun!"

Again, instinct took over. She couldn't let herself be captured. Her friends needed her. So did Mitch. Instead of surrendering, she grasped her gun by the barrel, stepped forward and swung it at his head.

The move caught him off-guard. He ducked, but he didn't avoid the blow entirely. The gun stock struck him on the shoulder. She could feel the reverberations all the way up her arms. She was pulling back for another swing when a dark form blurred her peripheral vision.

Mitch seemed to come out of nowhere. He moved behind the man, hooked one elbow around his throat and used his other hand to squeeze the angle of his arm tighter. The man struggled for only a few seconds, then went completely limp. Mitch released his sleeper hold and snatched the man's gun as he collapsed to the ground. He gave him a tap with the butt end to ensure he wasn't faking, then looked at Chantal. "Damn, I'm glad you're on my side."

She could barely breathe. Forming a coherent response was beyond her. Once again, the speed of Mitch's actions had shaken her. Yet it was her own actions that had shaken her the most.

"Are you okay?"

She shoved her wet hair out of her face and nodded.

"You were incredible."

She didn't feel incredible, she felt sick. She stared at the man who was stretched out on the ground. The poncho hood had fallen back. Rain beat on his closed eyelids and gaunt features. It mixed with the blood to form pink rivulets on the sides of his nose. The end of a ponytail lay along his neck. He looked lifeless, totally flaccid. She thought he was dead until she saw the slight rise and fall of his chest.

"Chantal?"

She returned her gaze to Mitch.

He stood tall and solid, in spite of the wind and pounding rain. His black jacket was gleaming wet, his hair plastered flat to his head. His expression was as hard and forbidding as the rock they were standing on. Yet his mere presence reached through her budding hysteria like a warm hug. It steadied her pulse. It brought her back to herself.

Her lungs finally started to work again. "I couldn't pull the trigger," she said.

"Just as well. Even with this rain, someone might have heard the shot."

"I was signaling you. I tried to warn you."

"You did great. I got your message."

"The message," she said quickly. "Did you send one? Did you contact anyone?"

"I reached someone in Bethel Corners."

"Sheriff Prentice?"

"No, a deputy named Hennessey."

"I know Al Hennessey. He's a good man."

"I'm not sure he believed me."

She glanced at the downed guard again. "I'm sorry you didn't have more time. He turned so fast, I didn't have a chance to hide."

"Don't worry about it. Even if he hadn't seen you, he would have raised the alarm when he got back and found out it wasn't his buddy he'd seen at the chopper." He cupped her shoulder and gave a firm squeeze. "We can't linger here, Chantal. We need to move."

Her stomach started to roll as she thought of the danger they were still in and of what might have happened if she hadn't acted. She tried to concentrate on the moment the way Mitch was. She looked around for the flashlight she'd thrown, then went to pick it up. "I broke the bulb."

"It doesn't matter if it works or not. We can't leave any traces or they'll know someone else has been here."

She pointed at the motionless form on the ground. "What about him?"

"We can't leave him, either," Mitch said. "He could come in useful." He engaged the safety on the man's gun and held it out to her. "I'll need you to carry this, if it's not too heavy for you."

It wasn't the weight that bothered her, but this was no time to indulge herself in a belated bout of squeamishness. She lifted aside her wet hair and looped the strap over one shoulder, then did the same on the other shoulder with her own weapon.

Meanwhile, Mitch retrieved his cane, grabbed the unconscious man's arm and in one smooth motion hoisted him across the back of his shoulders in a fireman's carry.

"What are we going to do with him?" Chantal asked.

"I'm not sure," he said, starting across the hill. "But we've made a good team so far. We're bound to think of something."

Lewis glanced at his watch, walked to the office door and peered down the hall. "Where the hell is Bamford?"

Taddeo was leaning against the wall and using his knife to pick at something under one of his fingernails. "Last I saw him, he was going outside."

"When?"

"Must have been an hour ago. He was bitchin' like crazy about having to do Benny's shift."

"He's not responding to his walkie-talkie."

"I bet he's off having a smoke someplace out of the rain."

Lewis agreed. The men's attitude toward discipline was sorely lacking. He had to remind himself they had other valuable attributes, starting with their viciousness.

"You want me to go look for him?" Taddeo asked.

Lewis considered the offer for only a moment. It wasn't like any of these men to volunteer for extra duties. Taddeo must be hoping for a chance to take a break himself. With Brown still out of commission, sending an extra man to chase down the AWOL Bamford would leave them even more shorthanded.

He dismissed the suggestion with a flick of his hand. The computer link with the Petherick head office was up and working. Bamford was no longer essential to the plan, so they could do without him for now. Lewis would deal with him when he showed up. "Bring me Petherick and Whitby," he ordered.

Taddeo stored his knife in his belt and pulled his ski mask back on. It wasn't long before the two executives were herded into the room. Like the rest of the hostages, they still wore what they'd had on when they'd been rounded up the day before. Graham Petherick didn't look like the head of a billion-dollar company. With his feet bare and his rumpled pajamas stretched over his potbelly, he looked like a helpless old man. In a gesture of solidarity, he'd given his robe to Jim Whitby to cover his underwear, but the garment hung like a hand-me-down on the much-smaller frame of the company comptroller. The overall effect of the pair of them was comical.

That suited Lewis just fine. A demoralized hostage was less likely to cause trouble. His own ski mask firmly in place, he pointed to the computer. "Time to confirm the shipping orders, Petherick."

He sat in the chair, but didn't lift his hands to the

keyboard immediately. "I want a guarantee that you'll keep your word," he said.

"You're in no position to make demands."

"Then as a gesture of goodwill, let the women and the boy go. I've done what you've asked. You don't need them."

"Let them go where?" Lewis asked. "For a stroll down the road? Have you forgotten where we are?"

"I'll call in my pilot. He'll do what I tell him, no questions asked."

"You're a businessman, Petherick. You should know better than to insult the intelligence of someone you're doing business with. The women would talk the instant they were released, and then what would happen to our deal?"

Petherick spoke quickly. "I can make you a better deal. How much are you being offered for that shipment? I'll top it. We don't need to take this any further."

Lewis pulled his pistol from the holster at his waist. Rather than aim it at Petherick, he pressed the muzzle to Whitby's temple. "You're the company comptroller, correct?" he snapped.

Whitby's first reaction was indignant surprise. When Lewis didn't remove the gun, his face paled. "P-please. I've been cooperating. Don't hurt me."

Yes, he'd been cooperating more than Petherick knew, but it wouldn't hurt to remind them both who was in charge. "You know the balance sheet better than your boss. How much cash can he produce within forty-eight hours?"

"I have a wife and three children. My youngest is sick. They depend on me."

Lewis cut off the man's whining with a warning glare. "Answer the question."

"It's difficult to place a dollar value on our assets. Our financing is a fluid entity. In order to raise a significant amount of funds—"

"Meaning you don't have a lot of cash."

Whitby looked at Petherick. "I'm sorry, Graham. I'm not risking my life to say what you want. I have to tell the truth."

"There's my answer," Lewis said, withdrawing the gun. "The merchandise will be sold to the highest bidder. That's not going to be your boss."

Petherick's jaw twitched. "Please. I'm begging you to reconsider. You're an American. Think of the tragedy our country has already been through. You know what could happen if those weapons fall into the wrong hands."

Appealing to Lewis's patriotism was the wrong strategy. He'd given his best years to his country, and it had turned its back on him. He'd worked hard coordinating their shipments of supplies, and he'd deserved more than they'd paid him. No one would have missed those few crates of goods that he'd sold, yet the army had called it theft and had thrown him out with a dishonorable discharge. To add to the insult, the psych profile the army quacks had done on him had dogged him even after he'd left. He had a right to collect everything he was owed.

"I know exactly what will happen," Lewis said. "The profits will end up in my pockets instead of yours. That's the American way. Now, I'll only say this one more time. I want confirmation that the shipment is being diverted to the destination I specified. Otherwise, I'll send Mr. Taddeo back to the lobby to choose a hostage who's more expendable than either one of you."

Taddeo pulled out his knife and caressed the blade with his thumb. "Let me bring the kid."

Ordinarily Lewis wouldn't have tolerated one of his men interrupting him, but it had the desired effect.

Without another word, Petherick set his fingers on the keyboard and started typing.

Chapter 9

"Knox made me help him. I didn't want to. You don't know that guy. He's crazy."

"You're not a good liar, Bamford," Mitch remarked. "I know you were promised a share of the take."

"Yeah, okay, but I'm not like the rest of his goons. I wouldn't have hurt her, I swear. I wasn't hired for muscle. All I do is work the computer."

"You know how to work an AK47, too."

Chantal waited by the door as Mitch led their prisoner across the main room. They had decided to bring Bamford—that was what he claimed was his name—to another one of the derelict cabins, specifically the one farthest from the Aerie. The location put them well out of hearing distance and past the range of Knox's patrols. It had been a long walk and Mitch's limp had become more pronounced the farther they'd gone. But at least Bamford had regained consciousness so he'd been able to walk part of the way on his own.

In fact, he'd been only too eager to cooperate once it was clear he was at their mercy. Apparently, Knox's men had no loyalty to their leader.

She shivered. Though the rain had stopped shortly after they'd left the crest of the hill, her clothes were still saturated. It wasn't only the soaked denim against her legs and the wet hair on her cheeks that chilled her. It was what Bamford had told Mitch on the way over here.

Knox wasn't trying to extort money from Graham's company, as she and Mitch had speculated earlier. He was after the weapons that the company manufactured. Not rifles or machine guns. No, Knox hadn't gone to all the trouble of seizing the Aerie in order to obtain a few crates of small arms. He was forcing Graham to divert an entire shipment of recently developed, ultra accurate surface-to-air missiles that the Petherick Corporation had designed for the U.S. military.

Far more than the lives of the thirteen hostages were at risk if Knox wasn't stopped. Hundreds, possibly thousands of innocent people could be killed if those missiles fell into the hands of terrorists.

Just when she had thought things couldn't get worse, they did. Again.

Chantal hugged her arms over her chest, striving for calm. There were another two days left. Somehow, they had to find a way to stop Knox and his obscene plan.

Her gaze moved around the cabin. It hadn't fared as well during the years of neglect as the one she and Mitch were using for themselves. Water dripped from the ceiling in one corner onto a darkening stain of rotten floorboards. There was a rectangular wooden table with two benches instead of chairs. The wood stove was a rusted-out hulk that appeared to be held together mainly by cobwebs. Dusk was falling early. Little light came through the boarded-up front window, although years' worth of forest debris had managed to find its way inside through the cracks.

Overall, the place was bleak and filthy.

But it made an excellent jail.

She found it hard to believe that they'd actually taken a prisoner. An enemy captive. It seemed bizarre, like something out of a game that kids would play. Cops and robbers. Cowboys and Indians. The captured prey brought back to the secret hideout.

Yet this was no game. It was a fight for survival in which the stakes had just been raised.

"What the hell is this place?" Bamford demanded.

"Your new home." Mitch used his gun to point to the doorway of the windowless room at the back. It would have been the bedroom, but there was no bed, only a pile of drifted leaves.

"Come on, man. I've been cooperating, haven't I? I've told you everything I know. We had a deal. You said you'd help me."

"I only agreed to protect you from Knox."

"You can't just leave me."

"I'll check on you in the morning."

"I've got rights," Bamford said. "You're supposed to get me a lawyer."

"You're confusing me with a cop. I'm a soldier."

"I've still got rights."

"You and Knox conspired in a potential attack on the United States, so this is a matter of national security. As far as I'm concerned, you're an enemy combatant and you have no rights."

"I can't stay here!"

"Would you prefer that I shoot you?" Mitch asked calmly.

Some of Bamford's bravado faded. He looked at the gun, then at Mitch's face.

Mitch's expression was pure granite. Chantal could see now that his ability to hide his emotions was a tool to him, as effective for establishing control as the weapon he held. To someone who didn't know him, he would appear devoid of feeling, fully capable of doing whatever was necessary to achieve his goal.

Bamford must have reached the same conclusion. "Hell," he muttered. "You're as bad as Knox is." Without further protest, he went into the bedroom that would serve as his cell.

Mitch swung the door closed, dragged over the table and tipped it on end to wedge against the door. He used one of the benches as a brace to hold it in position. Once it was secured to his satisfaction, Chantal helped him drag the other bench outside. Together, they braced the front door so it couldn't be opened from the inside as added insurance that their prisoner wouldn't escape.

Part of her was uncomfortable with the idea of penning up a human being, but she understood there had been little choice. For their own safety, they couldn't have let him go free. If Knox knew for certain they were still alive, he might try to hunt them down. In spite of Mitch's threat, she didn't believe he would have shot an unarmed man in cold blood. The only other choice would have been to bring their prisoner with them. If they'd done that, they would have needed to tie him up and gag him or watch him constantly—probably both. That would have drained their strength and diverted their attention from their priority, which was still to find help for the hostages before time was up.

Her mind turned to what her friends and Graham's people were facing. The image of the helpless hostages was a familiar one, because it had been haunting her for a day and a half. Added to that was an image of the destruction one of the stolen surface-to-air missiles could bring. She'd seen the aftermath of plane crashes on the news. The idea that anyone would deliberately cause such a thing was unthinkable, yet that's what could result from Knox's plan. The Aerie, a place of peace, was being tainted by his evil.

Any sympathy Chantal might have had for Bamford disappeared. She took a moment to get her bearings, then led Mitch to the trail that would take them back to their own cabin.

Mitch pulled open the door in the wood stove to add another piece of wood to the fire. The air had been too calm to risk building one the night before. Tonight the wind blew strongly from the northeast, so any smoke that didn't get swallowed by the damp air would be carried away from the Aerie. There was an outside chance that it would be detected, but Knox's men would have no idea where it was originating. Mitch's main concern right now was Chantal.

The only illumination in the cabin came from a candle stub he'd placed on the table. Despite the dim light, he could see that her shivering worsened and her lips and nails were devoid of color. Although she'd once again eaten every morsel of the fish he'd cooked, her energy was definitely flagging. Her suede jacket hadn't proved as good protection from the rain as his leather one had, and the chill she'd acquired had gone deep.

"I can do that," Chantal said. She picked up a piece of

the firewood he'd brought in. "You should be staying off your ankle."

It was true that he'd aggravated the sprain by carrying Bamford, yet he wasn't ready to rest. He ignored his discomfort and picked up the rope he'd brought from the boathouse that morning. He strung it between a line of nails that projected from the rafters above the stove.

"What are you doing?"

"Making a clothesline. You got soaked to the skin during that squall and you need to get dry."

"So do you."

"I was inside the chopper for the worst of it. I didn't get as wet as you did and my pants aren't heavy denim. They're not holding in the moisture."

"Well, don't worry about me. I'm fine," she said quickly. She closed the stove door and went over to the table.

"No, you're not. You said you took first aid courses. You should recognize that you're exhibiting signs of hypothermia."

"It's only October. It's not that cold."

"Chantal, I can hear your teeth chattering."

"And I can see you limping. Go sit down."

"Not until you take off your clothes."

His words fell into a sudden silence. He fastened the rope to the final nail and turned to face her.

She was looking at the floor and rubbing the outside of her right thigh. He'd noticed her do that before when she was uncomfortable about something. In fact, he remembered seeing the same gesture when she'd been a teenager. It didn't take a genius to know what it was that bothered her now.

"I'm not making a pass at you, Chantal. I'm trying to be practical."

She lifted one hand in a vague gesture.

"Our immune systems are already strained because of stress, poor diet and lack of rest. Neither of us can afford to get sick."

"I realize that."

He went to the bedroom, took the quilt she'd used the night before and handed it to her. "You can get undressed under this. Hand me your things and I'll hang them up."

"Then will you sit down?"

"Sure."

"You'll rest your ankle?"

"Absolutely."

"Turn around."

He almost reminded her that her modesty was misplaced since he'd seen her naked before, but that wouldn't have improved the situation. The circumstances were already too reminiscent of that other rainy night. He did as she asked and faced the stove.

The sound of her zipper made his mouth go dry. This was the second time in two days that she'd undressed in his presence, only this time he was aware she was doing it. He searched for something to say to take his mind off what was going on behind him. They needed to stick to business.

Chantal beat him to it. "We have to warn someone about that arms shipment," she said.

He cleared his throat. "Right. If we don't get a response from the authorities by tomorrow, I'll have to try sending another message."

"The same way?"

"We'll need to reassess the situation first. See how Knox is reacting to Bamford's disappearance."

"Wouldn't he be looking for him?"

"If he was any kind of commander, it should be a top priority. The best-case scenario is that with no evidence that an outside party was involved, Knox will assume Bamford fell off the cliff and drowned."

"And the worst-case scenario would be that he organizes a search and they find this cabin."

Yes, that was the worst one. There was no point alarming Chantal more than necessary. "They wouldn't have enough manpower to spare to look everywhere. We're likely out of their range."

"Knox sounds like a brutal man. I wonder if Graham's going to do what he wants."

"I suspect he will. He doesn't have many options."

"Wouldn't there be some kind of extra security measures when it comes to shipping weapons that are as dangerous as missiles?"

She was peeling her jeans off her legs now. He could hear the soft, sucking noise as the denim tried to cling to her skin. He curled his fingers into his palms. "Graham would be able to override them."

"It must be why they wanted Bamford's computer expertise. He would have to get into the Petherick Corporation mainframe to alter the delivery instructions."

"It explains their timetable, too. It would take more time to divert missiles than numbers in a bank account."

"Where are the missiles manufactured?" she asked.

Her voice had been muffled. Mitch pictured her pulling her sweater over her head. He rubbed his eyes in an attempt to curb his imagination. "What?"

"If we knew where they were coming from, it would give us an idea where they were headed."

"Petherick has several plants. The main facility is in Pennsylvania. My guess would be the missiles are headed for the coast, probably to a small harbor rather than a large port with container facilities."

"What makes you say that?"

"The port security wouldn't be as strict. There would be less activity and fewer potential witnesses. The vessel could be something as innocuous as a small freighter or a large fishing boat. It would be the easiest method to get the shipment out of the country."

"And to Knox's buyer," she added.

"Knox has a helicopter. He's probably planning to rendezvous with the ship when it's at sea."

"To get his money."

"Very likely. He'd want cash on delivery."

"He has to be stopped."

"One way or another, he will be."

Her feet whispered across the floor. She spoke from just behind him. "Are you really that sure of yourself, or is this more of your efforts to keep up troop morale?"

He blinked. She had extended her arm. It was bare. Her wet clothes dangled from her hand beside him. Without looking back, he took them from her and hung them over the rope. Apart from the wet neck and cuffs, the sweater was merely damp, but the jeans were waterlogged enough to make the rope creak as their weight settled.

She'd given him only her sweater, her jeans and her socks. She'd left her bra on. He knew she wore one, because her breasts were large enough to have made it obvious if she hadn't. He assumed she wore panties, mostly because she struck him as the type of woman who wouldn't go without. Unless she was trying to seduce someone. Then he could all too readily picture how she might wear a blanket with nothing beneath it.

Only, that wasn't his imagination.

That's what she'd done seventeen years ago.

Damn. There was nothing he could do to stop the memories this time. He pivoted to face her.

She had the quilt wrapped around her shoulders. It stretched all the way to the floor. She'd pulled her arm back inside so he could see nothing except the tips of her bare toes and the hand that clutched the quilt closed at the base of her neck.

Another image superimposed itself on the present. Instead of the old quilt, he saw a white mohair blanket. Her hair had been wet then, too, because she'd been at the cemetery yet again. When she'd phoned him and begged him to come over, he'd thought she'd just wanted a shoulder to cry on. Everyone knew she hadn't been handling her grief well. His sympathy for her had overcome his common sense, so he'd gone.

She'd met him at the door wearing nothing except that white blanket. Her face had been puffy from a crying binge. Her eyes had had a feverish gleam. She'd claimed she'd taken off her wet clothes and hadn't had time to get dressed again.

It could have been true. She might not have intended to seduce him initially. She could have dropped that blanket in order to get his attention.

She'd succeeded. She'd aroused the undivided attention of every inch of him.

I love you, Mitchell Redinger. I have since the moment I first saw you.

The words floated from his memory, sounding as vivid as if they'd just been spoken, yet the face in front of him was the woman's, not the girl's. Suddenly, he wanted to know whether she'd said those words to anyone else.

Of course, she had, he thought immediately. Life hadn't stood still for her any more than it had for him. She was an attractive, intelligent and spirited woman. Passionate, too. She'd said she wasn't involved with anyone now, but there could have been any number of men over the years.

It was a reasonable thought.

Why did it make him want to hit something?

She'd called him her crush. Her fantasy hero. Her feelings for him hadn't been real. They both knew it. The chemistry between them now was largely because of the circumstances. It didn't run any deeper than other natural, physical urges, like wanting to drink when he was thirsty or eat when he was hungry.

There was no reason for him to feel possessive. No justification for wanting once again to see that look of adoration she used to have for him. He especially had no right to wish she would drop that quilt to the floor and give him a second chance.

Only, it wouldn't be a second chance. Not really. It wasn't the teenager he remembered that he was interested in, but the woman. It was the Chantal who'd used a flashlight and a gun butt to fight off an armed man. The Chantal who'd stirred him to the point of insanity with one kiss. If she let that blanket fall and opened her arms in invitation the way she had the last time, he wouldn't be noble. He'd look his fill. Then he'd explore all the ripe curves and dips that he'd felt through her clothes and he'd make damn sure there was nothing to trip over on the way to the bed.

"You promised, Mitch."

He jerked his thoughts back to reality. He had no idea what she was talking about. "What?"

She pointed her chin toward the table. She'd put a boat cushion on one of the chairs. "Sit."

Beneath the aroma of mothballs that still clung to the quilt, he caught a whiff of roses. He inhaled slowly, indulging himself for a while longer before he finally went to the table. He sat on an empty chair, took off his boots and lifted his left leg onto the chair with the cushion.

Distance was a good idea. So was resting his ankle. Too bad neither held as much appeal as thinking about Chantal naked. "How well do you know that deputy?" he asked.

Chantal slipped her arm from beneath the quilt again to drag the remaining empty chair closer to the stove. She angled it partly away from him before she sat. "Do you mean Al Hennessey?"

"Right. The one I got through to on the radio. You said he was a good man."

She combed her fingers through her damp hair to hold the strands toward the heat. "He is. He was a cop in Atlanta before he moved to Bethel Corners."

That was encouraging. "He sounded competent. Skeptical, though."

"Anyone would be if they heard a story like ours. There are times I have difficulty believing it myself. Trouble like this just doesn't happen out here."

"One thing I've learned over the years is that trouble can crop up anywhere. Eagle Squadron usually shows up once it's already happened, so I rarely see the peaceful side of places."

"It's too bad you couldn't have seen the Aerie under normal circumstances. You probably would have enjoyed it."

"Very likely. That's one of the reasons I decided to join Graham's party."

"I'm sorry you didn't get more time to talk to Al."

"Don't apologize again. I told you before, you did great. I had enough time to identify myself and to give him my location. Would he take the initiative to check me out?"

"Oh, I'm sure he'd do that."

"Then you know him well?"

"He's a friend."

"Did you ever date him?"

She shook out her hair and pulled her arm back beneath the quilt. "What difference could that make?"

"Just wondering. There couldn't be that many eligible bachelors around here, and you used to have a thing about men in uniform."

"No, Mitch. I had a thing about one man in uniform. That was enough."

"Then you didn't date him."

"No, his wife might have objected."

He lifted his eyebrows. "He's married?"

"Yes. Sharon's my friend, too. She and the sheriff's wife run a charter float plane service. She occasionally ferries clients out here for me. Why are you asking me this?"

"Good question." He propped his elbow on the table beside him and leaned his chin on his hand.

"Well?"

"If I came straight out and asked you about your love life, you probably wouldn't answer me."

"I already did. I told you I'm not interested in having a serious relationship."

"You've *never* had one?"

The quilt tightened around her shoulders. He could see the folds where she was holding it in her fists. She opened her mouth and closed it a few times, as if she was wavering between laughter and indignation. "Mitch, I'm thirty-five years old. You're not seriously asking me if I'm a virgin, are you?"

Was he? That would be stupid. Unrealistic. *Possessive.*

"I was curious why you never got married, that's all," he said. "I remember you told me how you love the Aerie and the power of the wilderness and all that, but you're also a passionate woman. I wouldn't have expected you to remain single."

"I've been married, Mitch."

His elbow slid off the edge of the table. He straightened. "I didn't know. Your father never mentioned it."

"He wouldn't have. The whole affair was an embarrassment to him. You know how big my family was about keeping up appearances. He likes to pretend it never happened. He told everyone I was away at college during that time."

Her hands were still hidden, but he knew she wore no rings. He would have noticed. "You're not married now."

"No. I'm divorced." She curled her legs onto the seat of the chair and tucked her feet beneath the quilt. "Am I the only one who finds this conversation strange?"

His lips quirked. "I know what you mean. Two days ago I would have doubted that we could have had a civil conversation about anything other than the weather and your resort's 'rustic luxury.'"

She gave a quick grimace. "That would have been the über-polite mode you mentioned."

"I'd say we're past it."

"Being in danger has helped to put my personal concerns into perspective."

"That's why troops under fire tend to bond with each other."

"Is that what you've done with your men?"

"I'm fond of them, but I don't bond with them the way they have with each other. As an officer, I can't fraternize. I need to maintain some distance so that I can keep the mission objective my top priority."

"It must be lonely at times."

It was, but he rarely thought about it. "The good we do more than makes up for it. But the issue of rank doesn't apply to you and me," he said. "As you've pointed out more than once, I'm not in command here. We're a team."

"That's strange, too."

He smiled. "Who would have thought?"

Her gaze settled on his mouth. "Yes, who would have thought?"

"So, tell me, how long have you been divorced?"

"A little over fifteen years."

"Fifteen… When were you married?"

"Three months after you left."

Mitch's smile dissolved. So many questions popped into his head, he didn't know where to start. For some reason, the one that he asked was, "Who was he?"

The quilt tightened across her breasts as she lifted one shoulder. She'd probably intended for the shrug to appear casual, but she didn't pull it off. It was too stiff. "His name was Daryl Vaillancourt. He was the son of one of my mother's friends. You might have met him at one of her parties."

"Was he an officer?"

"No, he had been studying English Lit at Tulane but had decided to drop out around the time of my mother's funeral."

"He took advantage of you."

"We took advantage of each other. I was…needy, so I deluded myself into believing that he loved me."

Had she offered herself to that man the way she'd offered herself to Mitch? Damn! He couldn't let himself picture *that.* She'd been so fixated on him, he'd never considered the possibility that she'd turn to someone else. Or that the next man would be enough of a bastard not to refuse her. "You were still mourning your mother. You weren't thinking straight."

"That's completely true. I was looking for an escape. I

knew in my heart I didn't really love him, but I'd thought that once we were married and went away everything would magically be okay. The void inside me would be filled." She paused, as if deciding whether to continue. It was a while before she spoke again. "I hadn't learned my lesson well enough. I was still looking for a knight in shining armor when I married Daryl."

"I should have checked on you. I should have realized how vulnerable you were."

"Why? I wasn't your responsibility. You had your own concerns. Besides, I was so angry with you, I wouldn't have listened to you even if you had tried to stop me. I certainly didn't listen to my father. To him, Daryl was unacceptable because he was a free spirit and the antithesis of everything military. He was twenty-one and had just come into a trust fund that his grandmother had left him. That's why he'd quit school. We ran off together and eloped. I'd considered it romantic. God, I was such a fool."

The urge to go to her, to pull her onto his lap and hold her in his arms, was so strong he anchored his hands around the seat of his chair to stay where he was. He knew instinctively his sympathy wouldn't be welcome. Worse, it might stop her from talking. "But it didn't work out," he said.

"For the first year, I threw myself into pleasing Daryl because that's what I'd thought I'd wanted. In return, I forgot about my own plans for college and turned my back on my family. The more dependent on him I became, the more our marriage deteriorated. It got to the point that I began to dream of being rescued from *him*. That was when I finally had to admit to myself that I'd made a mistake." She hesitated again. This silence wasn't as long as the previous one. It was as if she truly wanted to finish. "So I left."

Damn, he felt the need to hit something again. No, not merely something. He wanted to punch the faceless Daryl.

Had he cherished the gift of Chantal's innocence, the way she'd deserved? Had he been aware she'd had far more to offer than only her body? No, probably not. Otherwise, he wouldn't have driven her to the point where she would leave after only a year.

Chantal was a long-term kind of woman. She took her commitments seriously. He could see that in her devotion to the Aerie. He'd seen the same character trait in her closeness with her mother…and in her determined pursuit of Mitch. The man she'd married must have been a self-centered fool. She'd deserved better. "What did you do? Did you go home?"

"To my father? No. I wasn't going to count on anyone else to fix my life. That's how I'd gotten into that mess in the first place. I needed to learn how to rescue myself. I took a job waiting tables and enrolled in a business correspondence course. From there, I started working in the hospitality industry. Then one day I answered an ad for a position at the Aerie, and here I am."

A log shifted inside the stove with a thunk. The branch outside the window scratched across the glass as the wind picked up. A draft blew past Chantal's drying clothes, stirring another whiff of roses.

Mitch could restrain himself no longer. He swung his foot off the cushion and went to squat beside Chantal's chair. He laid his hand on the quilt above the outline of hers. "I am sorry that I wasn't there for you," he said. "And that I couldn't give you what you needed. I can understand now why you had so much resentment stored up against me. If I'd handled things better, you might not have been so susceptible to Daryl."

Her hair had been drying in the heat of the stove. The strands fluffed over her shoulders as she shook her head. "It's funny. Yesterday I would have given anything to hear you apologize like that, and mean it. Today, it seems like ancient history."

He squeezed lightly. "The past makes us what we are now. I'm grateful you told me. It helps me to understand how you became such an extraordinary woman."

"I'm not—"

He stopped her by touching his finger to her lips.

She jerked her head at the contact and lost her grip on the quilt. It gaped open, exposing a lacy bra strap and the upper slope of her right breast before she managed to close it again.

Mitch told himself to ignore it. He would have, too, only he made the mistake of looking into her eyes instead.

Her pupils slowly dilated. Her nostrils flared, as if she were drawing in his scent as greedily as he was drawing in hers. "I should check on my clothes."

He rubbed a lock of her hair between his fingers. "They wouldn't be dry yet."

"No, but I should probably put them back on."

"Later." He shifted his weight to one knee, bringing his face level with hers. He returned his finger to her lips, not to silence her but to caress.

"This isn't a good idea," she murmured against his fingertip.

He traced the outline of her mouth, then touched the place beside one corner where a dimple appeared when she smiled. "I know, it isn't."

"We should be talking about what we'll do tomorrow. Make a plan."

He rubbed his fingertip along the tiny hollow above her upper lip. Her skin was warm. Her color had returned. That meant the delicate shudder he felt under his finger wasn't because she was still cold. "Mmm?"

"If help doesn't…come." She tipped her head toward him, her eyes half closing. "We need to do something ourselves to—"

This time he did silence her, but he didn't use his finger, he used his mouth.

Chapter 10

How could two kisses from the same man feel so different? Mitch's mouth was gentle this time. His lips settled softly over hers. If yesterday's kiss had been a conquest, today's was more like a…an affirmation.

Chantal couldn't understand why she thought that. She didn't know how she was able to think at all. The pleasure that spread through her body at the touch of his mouth was bypassing her reason, as it had before.

His lips felt so relaxed, so certain, as if there was nothing to prove. This was pure delight. He was giving her something she never would have expected from the take-charge man she was coming to know. Tenderness.

It moved her more than passion would have. It was what she needed to push away the memories she'd allowed herself to share. Somehow he must have sensed how much she needed this contact.

What was she doing? She wasn't beginning to believe

in their special connection again, was she? This was just the familiarity that arose between people forced to share the same foxhole. Once this crisis was over, they likely wouldn't see each other for another seventeen years.

Instead of making her pull away, that thought made her lean closer.

The quilt slipped off her shoulder.

Without breaking off the kiss, Mitch pulled the quilt back up and tucked it into place, then slid his hand inside between the folded edges and cupped her breast.

The caress felt completely natural, like an extension of his kiss. The possibility of resisting never entered Chantal's head. She inhaled slowly, lifting herself more fully into his palm. She was cocooned in warmth. The heat of the wood stove at her back, the heat of Mitch's mouth and hand…it was wonderful.

His fingers were long. The skin on his palm was hardened with the calluses of a man who handled weapons on a daily basis. There was strength in his touch, yet it was held in check. He skimmed the lace edging of her bra at the same time he teased the tip of his tongue along the seam of her lips.

She smiled and opened for him.

His lips stretched against hers with an answering smile. The kiss deepened. She barely noticed when he slid his hand to her back to unhook her bra, or when he tugged the straps down first one arm and then the other. His tongue stroked hers in a slow-motion dance, beside and around, sending tendrils of pleasure deep inside.

Still holding the quilt closed at her throat with one hand, she slipped her other hand free and lifted it to his head. His hair was bristly at his nape and temples where it was short, silky where it was longer. She tunneled her fingers through it, absorbing the smooth slide across her skin and the warmth of his scalp. The beard on his cheeks had an additional day's worth of growth since she'd last felt it. It changed from stiff to sensually soft. She closed her eyes, overwhelmed by all the textures.

Most of all, she was overwhelmed by the fact that this was Mitch. *Mitch.* The man she'd spent a good part of her adolescence worshipping.

She hadn't dreamed about doing this, though. Touching his unshaved beard, smelling the traces of wood smoke and the tang of sweat that rose from his clothes, feeling the scrape of a callus within his caress—none of that belonged in a young girl's fantasy. Only a grown woman would appreciate a grown man.

And oh, he was all man.

He lifted her breast in his hand, taking its weight with a gentle squeeze, precisely in the way that felt the best. She smiled and drew on his lower lip, popping it into her mouth so she could rub it with her tongue. He pressed his thumb to her nipple. She closed her teeth over his lip.

He groaned and pulled back his head, shoved the quilt aside and leaned over to suck her nipple into his mouth.

There was an edge to his gentleness now. Her pulse skipped and settled into a heavy throb. She unfolded her legs from the chair to ease her feet to the floor, then looped her arms around his shoulders. She didn't want him to stop.

He didn't. He nudged her knees apart and moved between her thighs. Pleasure blurred on top of pleasure as he used his mouth and his hands on first one breast and then the other.

Never had she felt anything so intense. Not even the mindless grappling in the boathouse had aroused the feelings she was experiencing now. It was incredible. Desire built with each kiss, each caress, until she couldn't breathe. "Mitch." Or, that's what she'd tried to say, but his name sounded more like a moan. She caught his cheeks between her hands and wrenched his head up to hers. "Stop. This is too much. I can't..."

His lips were moist. His eyes glinted. "Sure, you can," he murmured.

"But—"

"Let me do this." Holding her gaze, he placed his hands on her knees and coaxed them farther apart. "Please."

She shuddered as his thumbs slid along her inner thighs. Like his first touch on her breast, this felt right. More than that. Necessary.

His gaze never wavering from hers, he slid his hand higher.

The climax came as inevitably as her next breath. It flowed through her nerves like a wave of warm syrup. Thick and sweet. Delicious. It swept her out of herself, away from everything that had gone on before to a place where there was nothing but sensation.

And Mitch.

Only Mitch.

And that felt right, too.

Chantal could sense the light strengthening against her closed eyelids. For once, she wished that she had the ability to sleep in. Like Mitch, she'd always been a morning person. No matter how late she stayed up at night, her internal clock woke her at dawn. Today, it would be so much easier if she could stay asleep until noon. Or until all this was over.

This? Did she mean the nightmare with Knox and the hostages? Or the relationship developing between her and Mitch?

No, this wasn't a relationship. Neither of them wanted

one. They'd been clear about that yesterday morning, and she hadn't changed her mind. This wasn't even an affair, since technically, they hadn't had sex. Or at least, he hadn't. She, on the other hand, had enjoyed one of the most outstanding orgasms she could ever remember. Simply thinking about it sent a tight ripple of pleasure between her legs....

She buried her nose beneath the quilt. She couldn't believe how shamelessly she'd acted. What was it about this particular man that made her want to humiliate herself? Just when she'd begun to purge the bad memories of their past, she had to add some brand-new ones.

"Good morning, Chantal."

She went still.

"I know you're awake. I can tell by your breathing."

She opened her eyes. Mitch stood in the bedroom doorway, his big body silhouetted by pink-tinged light that filtered through the front window. He had his arms crossed over his chest and one shoulder propped casually against the door frame, as if he'd been watching her for some time.

The thought gave her another little ripple.

"Your clothes are dry," he said. "I put them on the trunk."

Not only had he been watching her, he must have come into the room while she'd been sleeping. How close had he been? Why hadn't he touched her? What would she have done if he had?

The questions were useless. She hadn't come this far in her life to start fantasizing about Mitch again. There was nothing romantic about their circumstances.

But what if there were? What would it be like to be in a real bed, with clean sheets against her skin and scented candles flickering around the bedroom? How would he look at her if she wore her lace-trimmed, satin nightgown instead of an old quilt? And how would he look if he wore nothing at all?

That part she could all too readily imagine. She pictured how he would appear, leaning against her bedroom doorway, maybe fresh from a shower, his skin gleaming with moisture, his arms crossed over his bare chest, his long legs and his hips and groin naked to her view.

Mmm, yes. That was an image she would love to wake up to. Last night, he'd been the one giving her pleasure. It would be only fair if she got the chance to return the favor.

"I thought I'd head to the other cabin to check on our prisoner."

She blew out her breath. It took her a few seconds to absorb the change of topic. As far as Mitch was concerned, it wouldn't have been a change. He wouldn't have known what she'd been thinking. Thank God.

Well, what had she expected? That he would greet her with a smile and another kiss, as if this were a normal morning-after and they were a real couple? That wasn't why they were here. At least one of them was keeping their priorities straight. "When?" she asked.

"As soon as we eat. I set up some snares last night, so it's roast rabbit today. We'll take any leftovers to Bamford."

"Give me a minute to get dressed and I'll be right out."

He didn't move. She couldn't see his face, because the light was behind him. She could sense the tension in his body, though. "Do you need some help?" he asked.

"No, thanks."

He still didn't move. "Okay."

"Mitch?"

"What?"

She made a twirling motion with her finger.

He turned his back to her but he remained in the doorway.

It was absurd to feel shy at this point, considering what she'd let him see—and fondle, and kiss—the night before. It wasn't as if she didn't trust him to stay where he was, either, since he'd quite effectively demonstrated he had an impressive amount of self-control. She sat up and yanked on her jeans. Denim slid over her thighs, and she remembered the warmth of his fingers. She put on her bra. Her breasts tingled as she remembered how smoothly Mitch had removed it.

She gritted her teeth. She had to try harder to control her feelings. It had been awkward enough yesterday to attempt a coherent conversation when she'd been taking off her clothes in Mitch's presence. It was ridiculous to get aroused by putting them back on.

"Did you sleep okay?" he asked.

She'd slept like a log. An orgasm was a very effective muscle relaxant. "Mmm-hmm."

"Before we start the day, I'd like to clear the air about last night."

She quickly finished dressing, then leaned over to put on her shoes. "Mitch, I'd prefer not to talk about it."

"We need to."

"Why? There's really nothing to say. It was a mistake."

"Another one."

She remained bent over, her chest pressed to her legs, her gaze on her shoes. "Yes, all right, another mistake, but I hope you're not leading up to another apology."

"What if I am?"

"Then I would feel cheap."

Grit scraped against the wood floor. The tips of his boots and his cane came into her range of vision. "Chantal, no."

"Kissing you the other night was crazy enough, but I don't do one-night stands, Mitch. I don't have sex with strangers, or do partial sex, or whatever you want to call it. That's just not me, regardless of the circumstances, and I can't pretend that I'm cool with it."

"The same goes for me. We're working as a team, but I also consider you a woman in my care. You asked me to stop and I didn't. I can't excuse that."

But he *had* stopped, she thought. Well, sort of.

"Although, you're wrong about one thing," he continued. "You and I are not strangers."

"Yes, we are. Our paths might have crossed in the past, but to be realistic, we met as adults only two and a half days ago."

"We've been getting to know each other pretty fast since then."

"Only because we've been thrown together." She frowned at her shoelaces. She wasn't a girl, she was a mature woman. Why was she having trouble tying a simple bow? "We're still from different worlds, Mitch. Once this crisis is over, whatever the outcome, you'll go back to your life and I'll stay in mine. I don't want a… complication."

"You mean a relationship."

"That's right."

"Neither do I."

"Then we understand each other."

"Sure. We got it all straight yesterday." He stroked her hair. "But I still can't keep my hands off you," he said softly. "Doesn't make much sense, does it?"

Her laces blurred. Why did he have to sound like that, as if he cared? Next, she was going to start taking his attention personally again. She would build a whole make-believe world in her head where Major Mitchell Redinger loved her. Then, if she wasn't careful, the old feelings would begin to unfold in that hidden corner of her heart where she'd tucked away her love for him a lifetime ago...

No! She was not going to go there. She'd worked too hard to rebuild her life the last time she'd fallen for him. "We can't allow this...physical attraction to distract us," she said. "We need to stick to business."

"You want to focus on the mission."

"Yes. Let's call it that. You said you're going to check on Bamford."

"Right."

"I want to ask him about my friends."

"I have some questions for him, too."

"Okay. We'd better get started."

He placed his hand beneath her elbow to draw her to her feet. "For what it's worth, Chantal, I wasn't going to apologize about last night. Right or wrong, I enjoyed myself too much."

She put her hand on his chest to steady herself. Or so she pretended. The truth was, she wanted to touch him. Her gaze fell on the sprinkling of black hair that showed at the neckline of his sweatshirt. The idea of seeing him naked popped into her head once again. "Saying that doesn't help us focus on the mission, Mitch."

"No. Neither would kissing you again, would it?"

"Definitely not."

His grip on her elbow tightened. His chest rose and fell with a series of deep breaths. It was a full minute before he released her arm and turned for the door.

Chantal flexed her fingers and let her hand fall to her

side. It took much longer than a minute before Chantal could convince herself she was relieved.

The bush was dripping wet from the previous day's rain. The hems of their pants grew dark with moisture as they moved along the overgrown trail, but neither of them commented on it. In fact, Mitch was unusually quiet. Chantal placed her feet carefully to minimize the noise of her footsteps. She concentrated on her surroundings. Aside from the normal bird calls and rustles from what were probably squirrels or other small animals, the woods were silent.

She moved a pace closer to Mitch. "Have you heard anything over the walkie-talkie about a search for Bamford?"

"Knox put a man on it just before dawn."

"Oh, no."

"It sounded as if he was sticking close to the Aerie and its immediate surroundings, but we do need to stay alert."

She curled her fingers around the strap of the gun she carried. She continued to doubt whether she would be able to pull the trigger, but it did make a good club. "I had hoped that Al would have shown up by now."

"I haven't seen any sign of your deputy or any reinforcements he might have brought. Either they're here and they're getting into position, or your friend decided I was a crank after all."

"I hope that's not the case."

"I'll have to try contacting someone else."

"With extra men looking around, it would be more risky."

"Since Bamford's neutralized, they've got one less. We can chart their movements."

"We never discussed what we'll do if help doesn't come."

"That's right. We didn't." He pushed his way past a low-hanging branch and held it aside for her. "As I recall, you wanted to last night, but we got distracted."

Heat rose in her cheeks. Distracted? That was one way to put it. "How many men do you think Bamford's cabin could hold?"

"What did you have in mind?"

"Since we managed to capture him, it stands to reason that between the two of us we could get more."

"You want to take more prisoners?"

"Why not?"

His mouth twitched. "We're fresh out of flashlights. The next guy might not go down as easily as Bamford did."

She swatted him across the chest. "Don't laugh at me. I'm serious."

He let go of the branch and caught her hand. His face sobered. "We might be able to take a few more, but I'm concerned that Knox could start retaliating against the hostages if he thinks someone's picking off his men."

"Oh. I hadn't thought of that."

"If we make a move, it has to be decisive. We'll need to go after Knox himself."

"How?"

"I'd have to infiltrate the Aerie."

He'd said it with the same matter-of-fact tone he always used when he discussed strategy. As if it would be simple. Easy. The very idea made her stomach roll. "That would be dangerous."

"There's still a day and a half left before Knox's deadline. That's plenty of time for help to show up." He lifted her knuckles to his mouth. "And I wasn't laughing at you, Chantal. I admire your courage."

"I'm not brave."

"You are. You've got a lot of your father in you."

She tugged her hand free from his grasp. "Don't say that."

"It's a compliment. You have the same analytical mind as the general. Even though you've had no military training, you have a quick grasp of what needs to be done. You have a sense of fairness, but you're no pushover. You would have made an excellent officer."

"Mitch—"

"Which makes your dislike of the army all the more difficult for me to understand."

"It's not important."

"It is to me. The army's my life. It's where I live and who I am. I'd like to know why you hate that."

"Maybe 'hate' was too strong a word."

"Your feelings *are* strong. Otherwise, you wouldn't have eloped with a man like Daryl. You said he was the antithesis of everything military. That must have been one powerful aversion you were acting on."

For a man as bright as Mitch, she was surprised he hadn't figured out that explanation on his own. One of the main reasons she'd chosen Daryl was because she'd been reacting against everything that was *Mitch*. She'd chosen his total opposite, a man she'd believed was a laid-back, romantic dreamer, someone who wasn't concerned with his career or worried about doing the honorable thing. By marrying Daryl she'd thought she'd be safe from getting her heart broken again.

In a way, it had worked. Most of her heart had still belonged to Mitch.

She stepped back. "We've talked about me more than

enough. I want to know about you. Why do you love the army?"

He lifted one eyebrow. It was clear that he knew she was avoiding his question, but he let it pass. "Maybe 'love' is too strong a word," he said, echoing what she'd told him.

"You said it was your life."

"It is. I think I was born to be a soldier. Did you know that my father was one as well?"

She nodded. "He was a sergeant, wasn't he?"

"That's right." Mitch turned. They resumed walking along the trail. He kept his voice pitched low so it wouldn't carry far. "He served in 'Nam. It was all his stories of the incompetent shake-and-bake officers he'd met there that made me decide I could do better."

"He must have been proud of you. You're a good leader."

"I have good men."

She smiled at the way he'd immediately deflected her compliment. "Are they all as devoted to the life as you are?"

"Most of them. Some more than others."

"I'm surprised you would tolerate anything less than total loyalty."

"No one could doubt their loyalty. I meant the dynamic of the team's been changing since a few of the men got married. They never let their home life interfere with their duty, though."

Her smile faded. That was one of the reasons she disliked the army. Her father had always put his duty before his family. She understood it was part of the responsibility he'd assumed when he'd chosen to serve his country, but he'd been blind to the effect it had had on his wife and daughter. "Was that how it was when you were married, Mitch?"

He walked a few paces in silence.

She should let the subject drop. She shouldn't be making it more personal. She certainly shouldn't be asking about his love life, or his former love life. Yet she persisted anyway. "I answered all your questions last night," she said. "It would be fair if you reciprocate in kind."

"Reciprocate in kind," he repeated. "You're getting polite again."

"Well?"

"Dianne understood my job. She supported me a hundred percent."

"What about her? Did you support her in what she wanted?"

"Every chance I got. She was a ceramic artist, and she did amazing work. Two years after we'd settled at Bragg we pooled our savings so she could open her own gallery. Our careers and our personalities balanced each other, so if you're trying to ask about my marriage, it was good. Each year with her seemed better than the one before."

If Chantal felt a twinge of jealousy, it was overpowered by sadness for Mitch. He'd managed to find the kind of love that she'd once sought, and she was glad that he'd been happy, even if it hadn't lasted. "You must miss her."

"I do. I had taken my men on a training exercise when I'd heard she'd been in an accident. By the time I reached the hospital, she was gone."

"Mitch. I'm so sorry."

"It was…a bad time."

"Losing someone you love is never easy. It leaves a hole."

"Yeah." His steps slowed. "I tracked down the bastard who'd hit her. He'd been drunk. He'd thought he'd hit a deer. So I gave him more of a chance than he gave her and I used my fists instead of a two-ton pickup truck. I knew dozens of ways to kill a man, but I wanted him to suffer first."

She thought of the bouts of violence that Mitch had displayed over the past few days. They had been brief and to the purpose. She had trouble picturing him out of control. "Grief can make us do things we otherwise wouldn't."

"That's right. You would know."

"Yes, and we both remember what I did, but we're talking about you. I know you didn't kill him."

"Why are you so sure?"

She thought about that. She was the one who'd claimed they were strangers, yet she was positive he couldn't have used his combat skills to murder anyone. Why? "Because of your honor," she said. "The code you live by. You wouldn't have violated that, regardless of the provocation."

"I came damn close. Then I thought about a mission that was coming up. I couldn't let my men down. And once it was over, there was always the next mission, or a new guy to train. After a while, it did get easier."

"You filled the void in your heart with your work."

"That's right. It became my life."

"The army became your sanctuary."

He stopped at the edge of a stream and looked at her over his shoulder. "That's a strange choice of word."

Perhaps to him. She'd chosen it because that was how she thought of the Aerie. A sanctuary not of physical safety, but emotional safety. In his own way, Mitch had done the same thing that she had. "Does it fit?"

The roar of the helicopter took them both by surprise. It had been flying low, so they didn't hear it approach until it was almost overhead. The helicopter passed so close to the treetops that the backwash from the blades knocked down a shower of water droplets.

Chantal tipped her head back, her heart soaring. "Mitch, they've come!" she cried. "They're..."

The words died on her lips. The fuselage she glimpsed through the trees was solid, dull black with no markings. It wasn't help. It was Knox.

Mitch grabbed her by the waist and spun her beneath the nearest tree. He swung his gun to his shoulder and sighted on the helicopter. Before he could fire, it disappeared, dragging the noise of its engine behind.

"They're heading for the lake!" he yelled. He turned to follow. "Stay there, and keep under cover!"

Remaining behind wasn't an option as far as she was concerned. She grasped her own gun to keep it from banging into her hip and ran after Mitch.

He moved quickly, in spite of his bad ankle. He used a gait that was part hop, part vault, employing his cane to propel him forward. By the time she caught up to him, she could see the gleam of water beyond the trees.

He scowled when he saw her but didn't waste time arguing. He motioned her behind him and continued forward. As they drew closer to the shore, she noticed the lake wasn't empty. A small, yellow plane was taxiing toward a bay a few miles to the east, its fat pontoons bobbing on the water.

"That looks like Sharon's Twin Otter!" she said.

"Sharon?"

"The deputy's wife. She must have brought him here to have a look! He did come through! Mitch—"

A plume of water shot from the surface in front of the plane. Another one burst even closer. The Twin Otter exploded into a ball of smoke and fire. Debris cartwheeled across the lake. Flames shot through what was left of the fuselage.

Chantal was too numb to scream. She could do nothing but watch in horror as the shell of her friend's yellow plane rolled to one side, tipped on end and slipped under the water.

The black helicopter circled the wreckage twice, hovered above a patch of burning fuel, then headed for the north end of the lake. It was lost from sight behind the trees. A minute later, more smoke billowed into the sky.

She didn't need a map to pinpoint its location. It came from the place where the Waterfalls Resort was located.

No. Where it used to be. She knew in her bones that it was gone. Just like the plane.

This couldn't be happening. Mitch had warned her they might not find any help at Waterfalls. He'd guessed that Knox had gotten to them. Now she could see for herself that he'd been right. The evil that had taken over the Aerie was already spreading. She started to shake.

Mitch slung his gun over his shoulder and pulled Chantal into his arms. "It'll be okay," he said.

"How? They killed…blew up…I don't know how many innocent people. Right in front of our eyes. Sharon and Al never had a chance. Neither would Bob or anyone with him. Knox is a monster. How can we hope—" Her throat closed. She thumped her fist against his chest once, then turned her face into his neck.

The nightmare continued to get worse. There would be no help coming. They were on their own. She fought to hang on to her hope, but there wasn't enough left.

So she hung on to Mitch instead.

Chapter 11

Lewis strode across the lobby. His ears rang from the screams. The men who were supposed to be guarding the hostages had gotten slack and had allowed some of the women to get next to the front windows. As a result, they'd had a bird's-eye view when Hillock had taken out the plane.

It had sent them into hysterics.

Lewis pointed his pistol at the ceiling and fired four quick rounds.

One of the overhead lights shattered. Pieces of glass fell to the floor. There were a few startled squeals before the room finally went silent.

He aimed the gun at the women. "Get away from the window. Now!"

They were frozen in place. Their sobbing had stopped, but one of the Petherick executives still had her mouth open. She was gasping for air like a beached fish.

Lewis wasn't in the mood to be patient. He fired into the floor. The shot kicked up a cloud of wood slivers. "Move!"

The cook's wife, Tyra, ran to put her arm around the shoulders of the gasping woman. She led her back to the cluster in front of the fireplace. Lewis motioned with his gun, and the other Petherick woman scurried after them.

Taddeo took the red-haired college girl by the arm and hauled her back toward the rest, but he was helping himself to a handful of her breast along the way. The girl's brother lunged for him. Taddeo swatted him aside, sending him skidding across the floor and into a coffee table. The girl spun from his grip and turned on him with her nails. He tossed her to the floor beside her brother.

The men were getting as restless as the hostages. Lewis snapped an order at Taddeo, who retreated to a position beneath the gallery stairs. Meanwhile, one of the colonels rocked forward and got to his feet. Like the other army men, he still had his wrists bound in front of him with bundling ties. His hands were likely useless by now due to lack of blood circulation, but Lewis wasn't taking any chances. Their bonds would remain until the end. He aimed his pistol warningly at the colonel's midriff. The man looked at him stonily, then went to sit amid the crying women.

Lewis sneered behind his ski mask. Wasn't that just like an officer, showing gallantry in the face of death. He waited until he was satisfied that order had been restored, then moved outside to the deck. He went to the railing at the top of the staircase and looked over the empty lake.

The plane had been a nasty surprise. Molitor had reported seeing what looked like a canoe strapped to one of the pontoons. It was possible they'd been ordinary fishermen, flying in for the day, but it was also possible someone had come to snoop around. There was little left of the aircraft except some scattered debris and a haze of smoke that hung over the water. A breeze was already dissipating the smoke trail that had risen higher into the air. Soon, there would be no trace of the intruders, whoever they had been.

The cloud of smoke on the horizon loomed larger than the one from the plane, but it would burn out before long. Most of the combustibles should have been vaporized in the initial explosion. Besides, there was no one left who would raise an alarm.

Destroying the lake's other resort had been part of Lewis's plan all along. It would buy him and his men more time to disappear. Investigators would be so busy sifting through the rubble of both places, it could be days before they pieced things together. He didn't like having to alter his schedule. He'd intended to take out Waterfalls *after* he detonated the charges that had been set around the Aerie, but once the plane had been spotted, he'd had no other choice. Given the situation with Bamford, this was no time to take chances.

Lewis glanced at the trees that mantled the hill. They were thick enough to hide anything. Was Bamford really enough of an idiot to get himself lost? Or had he developed cold feet? Either way, he had become a liability. He pulled out his walkie-talkie. "Walsh, any sign of him?"

"Not yet."

"How far have you gone?"

He didn't respond immediately. "Walsh?" Lewis prodded.

"Why don't we let Molitor look from the chopper?"

The suggestion showed how shortsighted these men were. They'd brought a limited amount of fuel. They'd already used more than he'd calculated to chase those two hostages who had escaped the initial assault. They'd burned extra again today, which left them with little to spare for the trip to the rendezvous. They couldn't afford to waste it on a search pattern. "That's not an option," he said. "We clear out tonight. If he's not found before then, we leave him."

"Tonight? I thought we needed to wait another day."

"The timetable's been moved up. If you're not back by then, we'll leave you, too."

"Did I hear you right, Knox? You're changing the timetable?"

That voice had come from behind him instead of from the walkie-talkie. Lewis lowered it to his side as he turned. One of the men he'd left on guard duty stood at the door to the deck. He'd brought the hostage who'd served as their inside contact with him.

Lewis scowled. "What are you doing out here?"

Jim Whitby pulled the bathrobe his boss had loaned him more tightly around his skinny frame and walked forward. "The others wanted someone to talk to you about their living conditions," he said. "I volunteered."

In Lewis's opinion, the hostages had nothing to complain about. They had been fed each day. They were escorted to the bathroom at regular intervals. He'd restrained his men from getting too rough. "What's the problem?"

"The women wanted some privacy. Taddeo's making them uncomfortable."

"Tell them the next one who complains gets some privacy *with* Taddeo. Don't bother me with these details. We'll be moving out as soon as we confirm the ship is loaded."

"I thought you needed to wait until it was in international waters."

Why was everyone questioning him? He fingered his gun. "I trust you don't object, Whitby?"

The breeze from the lake strengthened. Whitby took a deep breath of the fresh air. "Not a chance. The sooner we finish this, the better. I haven't had a shower in three days."

"You're the one who wanted to keep up the farce."

"You have your exit strategy, I have mine. The money won't do me any good if I'm sitting in jail, but no one's going to suspect an innocent victim."

Lewis didn't respond. He couldn't respect someone whose betrayal could be so readily bought. True, Whitby had provided essential information, but if he could sell out the company he'd worked for, he could just as easily sell out Lewis and his crew. All the hostages would be sharing the same fate tonight, regardless of what this turncoat believed. He stepped forward and delivered a backhanded slap.

Whitby staggered sideways. "What was that for?"

"Your friends can see us. You want to keep up appearances, don't you?"

"You could have used some other way. You didn't have to get rough again."

"Consider it more exit strategy. Don't try to talk to me until I send for you." Lewis motioned to the guard. "Take him back inside."

Mitch took down the rope that he'd used for a clothesline, coiled it neatly and hooked it on the back of a chair. He paused beside the table. "That's looking good."

Chantal straightened, rolling her shoulders to ease their

stiffness. For the past hour, she'd been doing her best to draw a schematic of the main lodge, but she was no architect. The piece of charcoal she'd been using was no drafting pencil, either. Nor was the wooden tabletop the best surface for showing detail. "This won't be enough. You need me, Mitch."

"I need your knowledge of the layout."

"The Aerie is more than just a floor plan. I know it inside and out."

"Which is why I want you to teach me what you know."

She dropped the charcoal and wiped her fingers on her jeans. Mitch planned to move in on the Aerie at dark. He'd said he had no other choice. Even though someone was bound to investigate the disappearance of Sharon's plane, there was no guarantee they would get here in time. If they did come, Knox might deal with them the same way.

The day had seemed endless as she and Mitch had made their preparations. Now that dusk was approaching, the time was slipping by too fast. "I thought we were a team," she said.

"We are."

"And we're supposed to be focusing on the mission."

"That's what we're doing."

"So tell me, Major Redinger, if you were on any other mission, and you had a member of your team who was intimately familiar with the place you were about to—" she swallowed before she could continue "—to infiltrate, would you be leaving them behind?"

He leaned heavily on his cane as he walked to the bedroom. With the knife he'd been using to fix their meals, he cut a strip from the quilt. He wrapped it around the blade and slipped the knife and its improvised scabbard into the pocket on the outside of his right pant leg. "That depends," he said as he returned.

"On what?"

"If I deemed them unfit for duty, I wouldn't allow them to participate."

"Unfit?" She pointed at his ankle. "I'm fitter than you are. You hurt yourself again when you ran to the lake this morning. You're hobbling worse than ever."

"I've had worse. It'll pass. You, on the other hand, are not going to become a trained soldier by nightfall." He braced his knuckles on the edge of the table and leaned over to study her sketch more thoroughly. "Where are the air vents?"

"What?"

"For the heating system."

"There aren't any. We have radiant heating in the floors from an outdoor furnace. That's sufficient for cool nights. The fireplaces are vented straight to the outside. Those are only a few of dozens of details I know that you don't."

"I'll be fine. This is what I do for a living. I'll be able to concentrate better if I don't have to worry about your safety."

"*My* safety?" She picked up the walkie-talkie they'd been monitoring and set it down hard in the cold wood stove. "I'm not the one you should be worrying about. You heard what Knox said. His timetable's accelerated. They're leaving tonight. In case you've forgotten, that means they plan to kill their hostages. Thirteen innocent people, including a twelve-year-old boy, have only hours to live if we don't succeed. Not to mention the thousands of people who could be killed by the missiles Knox is stealing. We're their only chance. You couldn't honestly believe that I would be content to stay behind, do you?"

"Chantal…"

"Because if you do, then you truly don't know me at all."

"You told me you don't like to rely on anyone else, or to wait for someone to rescue you, but this is no time to let your pride overrule your common sense. Be logical."

"I could say the same to you. You're being too stubborn to admit you need my help. That's not logical, either."

He regarded the tabletop. He appeared to be memorizing the drawing.

She grasped his elbow. "You've said that I'm brave. You even went so far as to say I would have made a good officer. Was that only talk? Didn't you mean it?"

He straightened and turned to face her. For a while, he regarded her as intently as he'd studied her sketch. "I meant it, Chantal. I respect you immensely."

"Then it makes no sense to leave me behind."

"If you'd been anyone else, we wouldn't be having this discussion. I would be doing everything in my power to persuade you to come along."

"Is this because I'm a woman?"

"No. It wouldn't be the first time I've knowingly exposed a woman to danger. I've done it in the past. I've earned a reputation for doing whatever it takes in order to achieve the mission objectives."

"So far, you're only proving my point."

A muscle twitched in his cheek. "I should be grateful for your willingness to help, but I don't want to use you or to expose you to harm."

"Mitch—"

"The truth is, my desire to keep you safe has nothing to do with the good of the mission. I'm letting my personal feelings for you overrule my logic. It's as simple as that."

His tone hadn't changed. He sounded as matter-of-fact

as when he'd spoken about the Aerie's heating system. It took a moment for his words to sink in. "You admit you're being unreasonable."

"Yes."

"And unprofessional."

"Completely."

"Well, you'd better get over it, because if you leave me behind I'll follow you anyway."

"Why?"

"I just told you. You need me."

"Don't you trust me? Don't you believe you can depend on me?"

"Of course, I do. I'd trust you with my life, Mitch."

"It's your life I'm worried about."

"As far as I'm concerned, the safest place for me is right beside you. What would happen if I stay here and the man who's looking for Bamford finds this cabin? We've been walking around this area for days. The grass is beaten down. Anyone with any sense would be able to tell it's no longer deserted."

His gaze flicked to the window.

She pressed her advantage. "I wouldn't be able to defend myself, either, since I'd be tied up."

"I'd leave you a gun. You wouldn't let him tie you up."

"I didn't mean him, I meant you, because tying me up is the only way you're going to be able to leave me behind."

"You're really determined to do this?"

"As determined as you are, Mitch."

"It's going to be risky."

"I'm fully aware of that. I just care about you too much to let you do this alone."

He cupped her chin. "You care about me. What exactly does that mean?"

It was a dangerous question, one she didn't want to think about, let alone answer. She turned back to the table and picked up the piece of charcoal. "At least you admitted we're still a team."

"I think we make an excellent team," he said, moving behind her. "But let's get back to the other thing you said. You were telling me how you feel."

"It's just an expression. I'm worried about what would happen to you, okay?"

"I wouldn't say that I care about you."

"You wouldn't?"

He put his hands on the table on both sides of her hips to cage her between his arms. "That word's not strong enough for what I feel."

She dropped the charcoal again and rubbed her arms. "What you feel is from stress. Hormones."

"For sure, there's chemistry involved."

"We've bonded because of the circumstances. It's temporary."

"I know that's what we said earlier, but it doesn't hold up anymore, Chantal. I think we've both been in denial over what's happening here. It's not going to go away just because it's not convenient."

"Mitch, please. We already discussed this. More than once. Let's leave it alone."

He curled his body over hers to rest his chin on her shoulder. "Do you want to know something strange?"

"You mean besides the two of us having this discussion when we really should be planning how to stop a murdering monster?"

"Yes, besides that." He nosed her hair aside and kissed

her ear. "Remember the last time we saw each other? Before now, that is."

Of all the ridiculous questions. Remember it? She closed her eyes and looked at the image of the twenty-eight-year-old Captain Redinger that had been burned into her brain. His Patriots sweatshirt had been newer and cleaner than the one he wore now. The shoulders had been spattered with raindrops. His wet hair had shone from the lamp on the foyer table as he'd leaned over to pick up the blanket that she'd dropped. "Vaguely."

"I almost hadn't come over."

"Then why did you?"

"Because ten seconds before you phoned me, I could have sworn I heard your voice calling to me."

"I'm not sure I understand."

"I didn't, either. I figured you must have been on my mind because of your mother's funeral. Or because I'd been expending a lot of energy trying to avoid you."

She dipped her shoulder to dislodge his chin and pushed against one of his arms. "You don't need to go into that again."

He folded his arms in front of her waist to hold her in place. "Let me finish. The strange part is that I thought it was possible the two of us had some sort of connection. I'd tried to regard you as a kid sister for a while. That could have been why."

No. Oh, please, she didn't want to hear this. *He*'d thought they'd had a connection? That had been part of her fantasy, the make-believe world where Mitch had loved her.

"There's unquestionably something between us now," he said. "You said it's due to the circumstances."

"Because it's the truth."

"Possibly, but it doesn't explain why I feel so strongly

about protecting you, or why having my arms around you seems like such a natural thing to do."

Chantal covered her face with her hands. Her inner teenager wasn't celebrating this time. She was laughing. Mocking her. Thumbing her nose at the attempts she'd made to stifle her. "If it feels natural, it's because sex is a natural function. It's nothing special."

He tightened his embrace. The muscles in his forearms flexed, lifting her breasts. "This feels special to me."

"You're deliberately trying to distract me. You want me to stop worrying about the plan to go after Knox."

He turned her to face him, took her hands in his and pressed them to his lips. "Since I can't persuade you to stay behind, I'm going to be honest with you, Chantal. The odds of success aren't good. Even with your help, we'll still be vastly outgunned and outnumbered."

For an instant, she wished that he could have lied. Why couldn't he have called the situation a minor setback again, or assured her in that confident voice he'd used so often before that they'd find a way?

Yet that wouldn't be Mitch. He might sugarcoat the truth to comfort her, but he was too honorable to mislead her with false hope. "We still have to try. Neither of us could live with ourselves if we didn't."

"I swear, I'll do everything I can to keep you from getting hurt."

She nodded. "I know you will."

"Good, because I don't want to talk anymore. I can think of a far better use for my mouth."

There was absolutely nothing she could think of to say to that. She lifted her face. He lowered his.

The kiss tore through her nerves, kicking her pulse into a run. This was what she'd been waiting for all day. In spite of what she'd attempted to tell herself, from the moment she'd awakened she'd been longing to recapture the mindless pleasure of the night before. The difference was, this pleasure was bittersweet.

One way or another, her time together with Mitch would end tonight. No matter how thoroughly they tried to prepare for this attempt against Knox and his gang of killers, the chances of pulling it off were dismal. If by some miracle they did succeed, then everyone would be safe and life would go back to normal. That meant she would stay at the Aerie and he would return to his life at Fort Bragg.

If they didn't succeed, they could die. They both knew it. It was the reason they were so edgy. It was why they'd been arguing, and why this kiss was making her head spin.

She slid her arms around Mitch, holding on as hard as she could. In her kiss, she could express the feelings that she hadn't dared to put into words. The emotions she'd locked away in her heart so many years ago could never compare to the love she felt for him now.

Panic curled through her stomach. No. She couldn't be in love. She knew better than that.

The two of us had some sort of connection.

No! She grabbed his hair and yanked his head up before the old fantasies could get started again. "This is sex, Mitch," she said. "That's what we're feeling."

He turned his head to rub his teeth along her wrist.

"Don't try to make out there's anything more to it," she said.

"Why not?"

"Because that's all I'm willing to give you."

His gaze bored into hers. "Are you sure?"

She wasn't sure about anything except the overwhelming need to touch him. She pushed up his sweatshirt and unbuckled his belt. "You said it yourself. A team never functions well if there's tension between the members."

He grabbed her hand as she started on his zipper. "I didn't mean this kind of tension."

"Why not? We're both adults. We know where this leads. Sex is a great way to relieve stress."

"You told me this morning you didn't do one-night stands. Now you're saying you'd make love with me for the sake of team morale?"

Moisture flooded her eyes. She blinked it away. "No, Mitch. I wouldn't make love. Love has nothing to do with it. Why are you arguing?"

"I'm not."

"Then do you want to have sex or not?"

He pressed her fingers to the front of his pants. "What do you think?"

Her breath caught as she traced the hard length that strained against the fabric. An answering heat curled between her legs.

This time he didn't try to stop her when she lowered his zipper. He tilted his pelvis to make it easier. She shoved his pants past his hips, hooked her thumbs into the elastic of his boxers to pull them aside and took his erection into her hands.

He might have groaned. Or swore. Neither of them spoke again after that. She felt the touch of cool air, then the warmth of his fingers as he moved his hands beneath her sweater. Without letting him go, she leaned the top of her head on his chest. The pleasure he gave her blended with what she gave him. She watched him respond to every stroke of her palms and squeeze of her fingers, even the sweep of her hair as the ends brushed his skin. Her own arousal deepened with each increasing sign of his until the urge to do more became painful. She moved restlessly, her grip firming.

Mitch unzipped her jeans and pushed them to her thighs. She had time to kick free from only one leg before he grasped her by the hips and lifted her to the table. The friction of her sensitized skin against the wood made her gasp. She was ready, past ready. Without any more delay, he slid his hands beneath her buttocks and entered her.

It was primitive and powerful. It was what she'd offered him. Sex, that was all. There were no soft words or promises, no room for thoughts of the future, only a driving, pounding need. She hooked her legs behind his waist and lay back when he leaned over her, clasping his arms, hanging on as he finished what they'd started. She wanted to do this for him, to give him what he'd so generously given her the night before. She would find her own satisfaction in his.

Or so she'd thought. From out of nowhere, her back arched with a climax that knocked the breath from her lungs. It reached deeper, it took her higher than anything she'd experienced in her life.

If she'd been in love with Mitch, joining their bodies would have been the ultimate pact. A physical expression of their emotional commitment. It would be an occasion to savor. To celebrate. She'd had gauzy, romantic dreams of this moment that had included soft music, flower petals and satin sheets.

Never had she pictured an impulsive, partially clothed coupling on a charcoal-smeared table.

"Chantal?" he kissed her temple, then worked his way to the corner of her mouth. He pulled her to sit up as he withdrew. "Did I hurt you?"

"No, it was...good." *Good?* The word was far too tepid. She felt as if she were floating, her limbs too lax to move. Little sparks of pleasure continued to pulse through her body.

His belt buckle clinked as he hitched up his pants and fastened them. The sound set off another series of sparks. He ran his hands over her back and down her hips. "Your sweater wasn't much of a cushion. Damn, I hope you didn't get any slivers."

Her lips trembled. She wasn't sure whether it was from a laugh or a sob. No music, no romantic bed. No declaration of undying passion from her lover, only concern that she might have acquired splinters from the wooden table.

Of course, what else could she have expected from a practical man like Mitch? "I'm fine," she said. It was an understatement. If she'd wanted to describe her condition more accurately, she would have needed to purr.

The laugh won. She swayed forward to kiss him.

He smiled against her lips as he continued to skim his palms over her bare leg. He tugged the dangling leg of her jeans past her foot and dropped them to the floor. "I promised myself I'd take a closer look." Leaning over, he trailed kisses along the skin he'd just bared. "Next time, we won't be in such a hurry."

The sensation of his breath on her thigh sent an echo of pleasure between them. She tunneled her fingers through his hair. Music and satin were overrated. "Next time?"

"Mmm. I can't figure out how you can still smell like roses after two nights in the bush," he murmured, kissing the angle of her hip bone. He stopped midway to her right knee. His fingertip circled the patch of smooth tissue on the outside of her thigh. "What's this?"

He'd only seen her by candlelight the night before. Seventeen years ago, he hadn't taken the time to look at her then the way he was now. The pleasure faded. She wriggled away from his touch and slid off the table. "It's an old scar. It's nothing."

He scooped her jeans from the floor and paused to scrutinize her leg. He straightened slowly, his smile disappearing. "Chantal, that looks like a bullet wound."

Chapter 12

Chantal took her clothes from Mitch and turned her back to put them on. The sudden shyness she felt was absurd, considering what they'd just done. Yet like this morning, she felt too exposed. She zipped her jeans.

"The wound *was* from a bullet, wasn't it?" he persisted. "I've seen enough of them to know."

Automatically, she dropped her right hand and touched it to the denim over the scar on her leg.

"I've noticed you do that before," he said, placing his hand over hers. "I never knew what you were rubbing. Does it hurt?"

"No, it's just a stupid old habit." She twisted away and walked to the window. The breeze was scraping the branch across the glass again. She peered past it toward the lake. "We should probably start the climb up the hill if we want to be in position by dark."

"There's still plenty of time." He limped across the

floor, took her by the shoulders and regarded her soberly. "How did it happen?"

"It doesn't matter."

"It must, because you're trying to change the subject. You've done that before too, when something makes you uncomfortable. Talk to me."

"Mitch…"

"What we did just now was great, Chantal, but I'm greedy enough to want more. I need to know more about you than the smell of your skin and the feel of your body. Is that bullet wound the reason you don't like guns?"

If only it was that simple. "In a way."

"It looked old. You must have been a kid when you got it."

"I was six."

"Six? That's how old you were when your mother had the accident with one of the general's guns."

She'd told him about that incident two days ago. Was this why? Had she *wanted* him to guess, to put it together himself so that she didn't need to go back on her word? "Your memory is phenomenal."

"What happened?"

This was the point where she should lie. She'd done it for twenty-nine years. She'd kept the secret and had been a good daughter. She'd never told a soul, no matter how the sadness and anger had overwhelmed her. Even that final night, when she'd bared everything to Mitch, she wasn't sure if she would have shared this particular truth.

Would it have made a difference if she had? Would he have stayed? If he had, it would have been out of pity.

She raked her hand through her hair. A dusting of charcoal came off on her fingers. Her mother would have been appalled at her lack of grooming. Never mind having sex on a table, being slovenly was the bigger crime.

Appearances must be maintained at all costs. She rubbed her hand hard against her sweater. "I don't want you to feel sorry for me."

"I might feel sorry for the kid you once were, but not for the woman you are now." He drew her a few steps away from the window so he could brace one hand against the back of a chair. "I respect your strength too much for that."

He'd said precisely the right thing. She sighed. "It's a long story."

"Tell me about it. You said no one was hurt."

"I lied."

"Why?"

"Because I'd promised never to tell." She stopped. That had sounded like something a child would say. Her mother had had no right to extract that promise from her. She'd understood that years ago. She'd been cheated out of her childhood because of her loyalty and her eagerness to be loved. She couldn't be expected to carry the secret to her grave.

Yes, her grave. She could die tonight. So could Mitch. In light of that, her hesitation over this was as absurd as her modesty. She placed her hand on Mitch's chest, took a deep breath and said the words she'd kept inside her entire life. "My mother was an alcoholic."

It likely wasn't the secret he'd expected. His eyebrows lifted. "I'm sorry, Chantal. I had no idea."

"You couldn't have. No one did. She was terrified of creating a scandal. All she cared about was being the perfect officer's wife."

"She'd seemed happy."

"She tried hard to be, but she couldn't take the loneliness. My father was the center of her world. She was lost when he went away. When he was home, she threw all her energy into organizing dinners and cocktail parties that would help him advance his career. She cultivated political contacts as much as military ones. She wanted so badly to please the general that she made herself a nervous wreck each time she entertained."

Mitch laid his hand gently over hers. "Is that when she drank?"

It was surprising how easily the words were coming. They had been festering a long time. Like her memories of Mitch, maybe it was a good thing they were being purged, too. "There was seldom a time when she didn't drink. She used alcohol to take the edge off her nerves when he was home. She used it as a comfort when he was gone. Her manners were so ingrained, no one could tell when she was drunk. No one guessed. She hid it well."

"Not from you, though."

"No, not from me. I was what the current jargon calls an enabler. I loved her, and I wanted her to love me, so I helped her keep her secret. I cleaned up the messes she made. She trained me how to host parties so I could take her place when she was too inebriated to hide her condition."

"She was drunk when she shot you, wasn't she?"

Chantal nodded. He'd pieced some of it together. She hesitated, then decided to tell him the rest. "I was late coming home from school that day because I'd made friends with a girl whose father had just moved to the base. My mother didn't like being alone. She counted on me to keep her company when my father was away, and she was upset. She'd had more to drink than usual. She'd spilled half the box of ammunition before she'd managed to load his favorite Webley."

Mitch's hand tightened. "Wasn't it an accident?"

"Oh, she'd never meant to shoot me. That *was*

accidental. She'd been trying to shoot herself. The gun went off when I pulled it away from her head."

"My God," he murmured. "You were only six."

"I felt it was my fault because I was late coming home. I told the doctor I was playing with the gun. He was a friend of my mother's and went along with her pleas to hush it up. She didn't want anyone criticizing the general about his gun collection, you see. No one knew the truth, not even my father. After that, I never stayed after school to play with my friends. I made sure I was there to take care of my mother."

"You were only six," he repeated, his voice hoarse.

"It was the pattern of my childhood. Wherever we moved, everyone believed my mother and I were inseparable. You thought I had led a sheltered life. In a way, I did. I didn't dare make my own friends or join clubs or play sports because I was so afraid I wouldn't be there the next time she decided to load one of my father's guns." She slid her hand from his grip and moved to put the table between them. Now that she'd begun, she wanted to finish. It would be easier to do that if she weren't touching him. Things got confused when she touched him. "When I got older, I didn't date either, for the same reason. My only escape was my imagination."

As if he understood her need for space, he didn't follow her this time. "Someone should have helped you. Or gotten your mother into a rehab program. You never should have had to bear that burden on your own. Didn't the general notice something was wrong?"

"He was too wrapped up in his career. Like a lot of soldiers, he didn't show his emotions, and he was uncomfortable when anyone else did. If we hadn't moved so often, one of our friends might have seen through my mother's act, but transfers are part of the army life. We never stayed in any one place long enough to develop close ties. I was brought up not to complain. My father called me his good little soldier. Being my mother's keeper was my duty, and I did the best I could. I…kept her alive."

"You blame the army for the situation with your mother, don't you?" he said. "That's why you said you hate it."

"You're a perceptive man, Mitch. Yes, I blame it for what it does to people and what it turns them into. It started killing my mother long before that aneurism finally did."

"Chantal—"

"Don't," she said, holding up her palm. "I know how important the army is to you, and you're probably going to point out how illogical it is for me to condemn the entire organization because of my personal experience."

"No, I wasn't going to do that. Emotions aren't logical or reasonable. Once you feel something, it can't be explained away, no matter how much you might try. Or how inconvenient it might be."

She could tell by his tone that he was talking about more than her feelings for the army. He was referring to what he'd said earlier about the two of them.

A lump came to her throat. Maybe it was best to get all of this out in the open, too. "You're right. Emotions aren't logical. Because in spite of the unhappiness I went through in my childhood, in spite of what the military life had done to my mother, I once made a complete fool of myself over a soldier who turned out to be just as obsessed with his honor and his career as my father."

He shoved himself away from the chair. "How many times do you want me to apologize for failing you? I am sorry. If I'd known the truth about how deep your problems were—"

"Would it have made a difference if you'd known?

Would you have stayed with me? Taken what I'd offered you?"

He fisted his hands. He didn't reply.

"Of course not. You had your code of honor. You wouldn't have taken my virginity. You probably would have gotten me into counseling instead."

"I sure as hell wouldn't have left you to be a sitting duck for a jerk like Darren."

"Daryl."

"But the first thing I would have done is to have found your father and given him a good, swift kick for being so oblivious to the needs of his family. I would have told him that being an officer means nothing if he isn't a man first. That would have ended my career faster than if I *had* slept with his eighteen-year-old daughter."

The sudden vehemence in his voice startled her. "Then it's just as well you hadn't known."

"For me, yes. But you haven't healed. You're still carrying around the scars of what you went through in your childhood as surely as that one on your thigh."

"We all carry scars of one kind or another, Mitch. I told you about mine because..."

"Because you trust me. Because you realize we have a bond between us."

"No, because I wanted you to understand why there *can't* be anything between us."

"There already is. We made love, Chantal." He smacked his palm on the table. Charcoal dust puffed into the air. "Right here."

"No, we had sex."

"Why are you determined to make that distinction?"

"I'm trying to be realistic."

"You claimed I was the last man in the world that you'd want. It sure didn't seem that way a few minutes ago.

You're holding the past against me when you know damn well I can't change it."

"No, Mitch. The problem isn't the past. It's what the past made us. It's who we are now. I'll never again be that child who waited to be rescued, or that needy girl who was so desperate to be loved. I won't be dependent on any man for my happiness the way my mother was. I like my life the way it is."

"You're afraid of love."

"Can you blame me?" she cried. "From what I've seen of it, it brings nothing but misery."

"And so you hide yourself away in the North Woods and dedicate your life to people who won't stay with you any longer than a few weeks. That's why you love the Aerie. It's safe, isn't it?"

"Yes. It's safe. It's my sanctuary, just as the army is yours. You hide yourself in your duty and in dedicating your life to the men of Eagle Squadron, men you have to keep your emotional distance from and can't call your brothers or your friends."

"It's not the same."

"Isn't it? It seems to me we both have chosen to live our lives alone. You might talk about connections or bonds or having something special between us, but you don't want it to be love any more than I do. You know how painful love can be. Otherwise you wouldn't still be wearing your wedding ring."

He glanced at his hand. His jaw tightened. "You're wrong."

"I've seen you rub that the same way that I rub my old bullet wound," she said. "Don't point at my scars. You've got some of your own."

He braced his knuckles on the edge of the table and leaned toward her. "So where does that leave us?"

Her heart pounded. Her feelings were too jumbled to single out one. Except for a sadness that threatened to drown her.

She focused on the floor plan she'd drawn. The lines were blurred. *Other* lines were becoming blurred, too. She crossed her arms, reverting to the defensive posture she'd assumed on the dock the morning after he'd arrived. How could it possibly have been less than three days ago? "It leaves us where we started, Mitch. We need to work together to save the hostages."

The weather conditions couldn't have been better. The breeze that had come up at sunset had strengthened enough to move small branches and rustle the leaves on the ground, providing background noise that would mask the sound of footsteps. The clouds were thick enough to douse the moon when they drifted across it, yet not solid enough to leave Mitch blind. He was grateful for the break. They needed every advantage they could get.

A pinpoint of light bobbed through the trees. Right on schedule. Mitch tapped Chantal's arm to get her attention then pulled her against the open-sided shed that served as the resort's garage. She waited motionless beside him as the guard went past. When the light disappeared, she turned and led the way inside.

"There's a toolbox on the shelf at the back," she whispered. "I'm pretty sure there's a small flashlight in it."

His arm brushed her shoulder as he moved beside her. She stepped to her right to give him more space. The move was subtle. Under other circumstances he wouldn't have given it a second thought.

But now, it made him grind his teeth. She was avoiding

his touch unless it was absolutely necessary. A few hours ago she hadn't been able to get enough of it.

This was why he always warned his men not to get emotionally involved with a woman while they were on a mission. It split a man's concentration. It messed with his head.

Yet it also gave him a hell of a good incentive to make sure nothing went wrong. This was one of the reasons why some ancient tribes went into battle naked. Being vulnerable raised the stakes. There was no protection against even the smallest error. One instant of inattention would bring unimaginable—and very personal—pain. That awareness took the issue of survival to a whole different level.

He reached for Chantal's hand as they entered the deep shadows at the rear of the garage. Not because her guidance was necessary, but because he wanted—no, needed—to touch her. There was a fine tremor in her fingers. It could be from nerves or it could a reaction to him. Either way, she was holding up well so far. "Show me where the toolbox is."

Her hesitation was brief. She led him as far as the back wall and moved his hand to the left until his fingertips encountered smooth metal. She opened the clasp on the front of the box herself. The lid squeaked softly. "Try the top tray."

He found the cylinder of the flashlight immediately. It was much smaller than the one from the boathouse. The beam was narrow and weak but more than sufficient for his purpose. He played the light over the tools, pocketed a few screwdrivers and a roll of duct tape that might come in useful, then turned the beam toward the vehicles in the center of the building. They had settled crookedly on their flattened tires.

It was fortunate he'd disabled them himself. If Knox's men had done the job, the vehicles likely wouldn't have been left intact. He bypassed the van and the ATVs and went to the Jeep. "We'll use this one," he said. "It's got the highest ground clearance and the biggest gas tank."

She gestured toward the red fuel cans along the side wall. "What about those?"

"The Jeep's gas tank will give us more time to get into position." He handed Chantal the flashlight. "Here. Keep it steady for me."

She held one side of her jacket over the beam and kept it angled away from the open front of the garage. "Are you sure this will work?"

No, he wasn't sure. He would have preferred to have a satchel full of C4 and time-delay fuses. He leaned his gun against the rear bumper and got down on the ground. "Once the fire spreads to the upholstery and the oil around the engine, it's a matter of time and physics." He pushed the dry sticks he'd brought with him beneath the vehicle's undercarriage and extended his arms to arrange them in a pile directly beneath the gas tank. "The tank and the fuel inside will expand as they heat. Pressure will build up until something's got to give, either the metal shell or one of the connections along the fuel line. When it does and the gas leaks out, it should ignite."

"Like my truck."

"Yes."

"Except this time it will take our supply of spare fuel and the building with it."

"I'd guess we'll have ten, maybe fifteen minutes once I light this." He pulled up his left pant leg and unwound a strip of what was left of Chantal's blouse. He opened the cap of the gas tank, dunked the fabric inside, then used the branch that had served as his cane to poke the soaked wad beneath the wood. He pulled one end of the cloth past the edge of the bumper and added the cane to the firewood. He could have used its support, but he would need the use of both hands more.

"Did you learn that on *MacGyver*, too?"

He wanted to smile but couldn't. He could tell what an effort she was making to stay calm, and it moved him. She had no shortage of courage. She must have developed a deep reserve of it to get through her childhood. It hadn't been fair. Essentially, they'd started out the same, both being raised on army bases, but he'd seen by his parents' example what real love was supposed to be like. If only things had been different for her.

He couldn't allow himself to think like that. Otherwise, he might start wondering what would have happened if they'd met again under normal circumstances. If Knox had never arrived, if they could have taken more time to get to know each other and had talked more instead of skipping past the preliminaries and getting ambushed by passion, would she still be as determined to reject him?

Then again, under normal circumstances they never would have gotten past their initial, strained politeness. He wouldn't have had the chance to meet the real Chantal. She might never have challenged him to take a better look at himself, either.

"No," he replied. "I picked up this trick from Junior."

"Junior?"

"One of the men on my team. He can blow up anything." He reached into his pocket for the matches. "Ready?"

She held out her hand. "Give me the matches, I'll do it."

Mitch knew she hadn't wanted to destroy the garage when he'd first proposed it. It was understandable that she'd want to protect her property. She'd also grasped the tactical advantage of a diversion, though, so she'd pushed aside her own feelings and had supported his plan. Now she was willing to light the improvised fuse herself.

He had an overwhelming urge to pull her into his arms. Not because she was weak or needed rescuing, but because she was strong.

What he felt for her was more than respect. It was beyond caring. And she was dead wrong about the gold ring that he still wore.

"Mitch?"

But if he stopped to talk about it now, he could get them both killed. That was another good incentive for making sure there would be a later. He used his gun to lever himself back to his feet, took the flashlight from her grasp and gave her the matches.

Chantal pulled herself over the windowsill and dropped lightly to the floor. She closed her eyes to allow them to adjust to the darkness, even though her first impulse was to flip on a light and kick off her shoes. This was her bedroom, her private nest within the Aerie. The familiar stillness closed around her like a hug, a tonic, a reminder of what used to be normal.

"You okay?"

Mitch's whisper jerked her back to reality. She blinked. The air wasn't familiar. It stank of cigarette smoke. The bed was unmade. The book she'd left on the bedside table lay on the floor with its spine cracked. What appeared to be a ski mask hung from one of the bedposts.

She swallowed her revulsion, took the gun Mitch was holding out to her and followed him to her sitting room. They'd chosen to enter the Aerie through her suite because the window had been dark and easy to reach from the ground. Knox or one of his thugs must have found it convenient too, since it was close to the center of the building.

She should have expected this. It was why Mitch had insisted on entering first, in case the room hadn't been empty. She tried not to dwell on the evidence of intrusion. Earlier, they'd observed that the kitchen windows had blazed with light. So had the window in her office, which Mitch assumed had become Knox's command center. The entire Aerie was being violated, not simply her personal space.

He pressed his ear to the door that led to the corridor, then flattened on his stomach to look through the gap underneath it. He watched for a few seconds before returning to his feet and easing the door open a crack.

Chantal's pulse skipped. A large, ski-masked man was standing less than a yard away. His head was partly turned toward the other end of the corridor. Something glinted from his hand. It was a knife with a long, thin blade. Her mind echoed with the conversation they'd overheard in the boathouse, and the man who'd spoken about bleeding Henry…

Before she had an inkling of what he was about to do, Mitch pulled open the door. He leaped straight for the man with the knife. As he'd done on the hilltop with Bamford, he caught the man from behind and closed his elbow around his throat like a vise.

The man didn't go down as easily as Bamford had. He slashed at Mitch's arm, opening a gash in his leather sleeve. In response, Mitch hooked his bad ankle in front of the man's legs and pulled him off-balance, letting his weight add force to the choke hold. Within moments, he dropped the knife and went limp. Mitch held on another few seconds before he shifted his grip to the man's arms.

Chantal lowered her gun, only then becoming aware

that she'd raised it. She snatched the knife from the floor and pocketed it as Mitch dragged the man into the room. There was no need to bind him. His chest wasn't moving.

She choked down a wave of nausea, reminding herself this was a matter of survival. These men were ruthless. They'd already demonstrated their willingness to kill.

"Taddeo, bring Petherick and Whitby to the office."

The voice had come from the fallen man's walkie-talkie. Mitch tore a piece of duct tape from the roll he'd taken from the garage, picked up the walkie-talkie and pressed the button to transmit. He wound the tape around the device to hold the button down, then stuffed it beneath the man's body. "That's to jam their communications," he whispered.

She glanced at the open door. The body would be visible to anyone going past. "Shouldn't we move him?" she asked.

"No, he's bait."

She nodded as if she understood, but she didn't even try. It was clear that Mitch was in his element. He was doing what he and his men had been trained to do. She hung on to that thought. It helped her keep the terror at bay.

Orange light flashed beyond the window. The boom of an explosion split the air, sending Chantal's pulse off the scale. Their homemade bomb had worked. Flames shot into the sky above the trees. There was no turning back, even if she wanted to. At Mitch's hand signal, she flattened herself against the wall beside the open door while he took up a position in front of her.

Footsteps pounded down the corridor. Two men ran by the doorway, likely on their way to the rear exit. One slid to a stop. "What the hell… Hold up a second, Ferguson."

Mitch lifted his gun to his shoulder. He waited until the first man crossed the threshold, then pulled the trigger twice. He did the same when the second man followed a split second later. "Let's go, Chantal," he ordered. "And stay close."

She leaped over the toppled men and ran into the corridor with Mitch. He moved swiftly despite his limp. They had almost gotten past the back staircase when there was the crack of gunfire. Bullets slammed into the wall above her head.

She ducked as Mitch spun and fired. A ski-masked figure crumpled to the floor at the foot of the stairs. Another one appeared around the bend of the corridor. Mitch fired as he ran toward him, dropping the man in his tracks.

Distantly, Chantal heard the sound of raised voices and a woman's frightened scream. The noise came from the front of the Aerie. The hostages. She instinctively turned toward the lobby.

Mitch clamped his hand around her arm to stop her. "Knox first," he said.

He was right. They needed to use their heads. Giving in to her emotions could get everyone killed. This was why soldiers like Mitch—and like her father—preferred to bottle up their feelings.

She couldn't believe she'd ever criticized either of them for doing that. Right now, she'd give anything to have developed that skill herself.

Chapter 13

Lewis knocked his walkie-talkie against the desk and tried again. "Who fired those rounds?" he demanded. "What's happening?"

There was no response, only the hiss of dead air.

Another *boom* shook the floor. He glanced out the window. A second fireball billowed above the trees. It looked as if it had come from the garage like the first one. What was going on out there? The charges weren't set to blow for fifty minutes.

He shoved away from the computer, took his pistol from its holster and walked to the door. There was no sign of Taddeo or of Petherick and Whitby. The corridor echoed with the noise of raised voices. Some of the women had started screaming again, and he cursed as he stepped through the doorway. No doubt he'd have to sort this out himself, too.

There was no more than a scuffing footstep to warn

him. As soon as he walked into the corridor, he felt hot metal press against the back of his neck.

"Drop the gun, Knox."

Lewis didn't recognize the voice, but he recognized the tone of command. It was what he'd tried to emulate since he'd left the service. Shock held him immobile. Who was this? How did they get here? And where the hell were his men?

"I said drop it." More explosions echoed through the walls. "We've got you surrounded. It's over."

Damn, it sounded as if they'd brought a whole platoon. He opened his hand, letting the pistol swing from his thumb by its trigger guard. He turned his head to the side. At the very edge of his vision he saw a tall figure standing behind him and the gleam of a gun barrel. He let his own gun fall to the floor beside his foot.

The man toed it out of his reach. Lewis got a glimpse of long, dark hair as a woman darted forward to retrieve the pistol. He heard the rip of duct tape. His wrists were seized and fastened together behind his back. His ski mask was yanked off and he was quickly propelled toward the lobby.

Lewis could barely contain his rage. Someone must have talked to the FBI. He'd guess it had been Whitby. Or it could have been Bamford. That would explain his disappearance. The bastard must have made a deal.

But why would the FBI use duct tape instead of handcuffs? And where were the rest of them? He spotted Dodson still at his post beneath the gallery. The hostages were still confined to a clump in front of the fireplace. What the—

Lewis stopped moving just inside the entrance to the lobby. His men were still armed and staring at him. There were no other law enforcement people in sight.

"Tell them to drop their weapons," the man behind him said.

"Who the hell are you?" Lewis demanded.

At their voices, some of the hostages looked their way. They seemed as stunned as his men. Petherick and the cook's wife were the first to react. They rose slowly to their feet. "By God, it's Mitch!" Petherick said, grasping one of the colonels by the shoulder.

"Chantal!" Tyra cried. "We thought you were dead!"

The names hit Lewis like a slap. Mitchell Redinger, one of Petherick's army guests. Chantal Leduc, the resort owner. Those were the two who had tried to escape. They were supposed to be dead. He jerked to look over his shoulder.

The man behind him could never be mistaken for an FBI agent. He didn't look much like an army officer, either. He was scratched and unshaven, his hair sticking up at all angles. His leather jacket was ripped and he looked as if he hadn't slept in days. Despite that, the expression in his eyes was as deadly as the gun he held.

Lewis remembered him. He'd seen both of them through the window the morning he'd arrived. He shifted his attention to the woman who stood beside Redinger. She seemed to be in as rough a shape as her companion was, only she wasn't calm. Her hands were shaking, the barrel of the AK47 she held was swinging wildly. Her gaze glowed with a desperation that didn't appear completely rational. If anything, she could be the more dangerous of the pair.

Damn that idiot Molitor. He and Hillock should have landed the chopper to make sure of the kill. Lewis scanned the lobby for them. His gaze settled on Dodson. "Don't just stand there. Shoot him!"

Redinger hauled him sideways by the elbow, holding

Lewis in front of him and the woman while placing their backs against the wall. The gun barrel didn't move from his neck. Instead, Redinger released his elbow and used Lewis's own pistol to shoot Dodson in the arm.

Dodson screamed like one of the women and dropped his weapon to the floor.

"Who's next?" Redinger asked. His voice was as hard as the steel of the gun barrel. "Which one of you men is willing to shed blood for his commander?"

The remaining guards looked around uneasily.

"Dammit, you can take him!" Knox shouted. "This is nothing but a bluff. He's alone."

"Wrong," the Leduc woman said. Lewis heard the click of a safety lever as she brought her gun to bear on his men. "There are two of us."

Petherick lunged forward to scoop Dodson's gun off the floor. "Three," he said, shouldering the weapon expertly as he leveled it at Lewis. He should have looked comical, a gray-haired fat man in striped pajamas. He didn't. He finally did look like a man who had made a fortune manufacturing firearms. "Call them off, Knox. You're finished."

The thrum of a helicopter sounded overhead. Lewis glanced toward the wall of glass at the front of the Aerie. His first thought was that Molitor and Hillock were cutting out on him. But then a spotlight glared from the sky, piercing every shadow in the lobby. Light spilled over the deck and the rock slope beyond the windows. Figures moved at the edge of the darkness. They weren't his men. There were too many of them.

"Shoot the hostages!" Lewis ordered.

His men ignored him. They had seen what he had. One by one, they laid their weapons on the floor and raised their hands.

"You cowards!" Lewis yelled. "Idiots! Whitby, I'm not going down alone. You better help me!"

Petherick started and glanced at Whitby. "Jim? What did he mean?"

The moment he looked away, Lewis bent forward at the waist, jerked his arms behind him as far as his taped wrists would allow and grabbed the barrel of Redinger's gun with one hand.

He'd intended to wrench it from Redinger's grip, prove to his men he was still in control and show them how to fight back.

But Redinger didn't let go of the gun. Or the trigger.

Lewis's death was instantaneous. He never realized that his own action had fired the bullet that killed him.

Chantal's ears were ringing from Mitch's gunshot. The sound of his voice seemed to be coming down a long tunnel. Something warm trickled down her face. She lifted one hand from her gun to touch her cheek and discovered the warmth was from blood. Knox's blood. It had spattered all over her when the back of his head had burst open.

She gagged and dropped her gun, then scrubbed at her skin with her palms.

People came from every direction. They poured through the corridor beneath the gallery, rushed down the staircase and inside from the deck. Men and women in dark blue jackets that had FBI spelled out in large letters on the back converged on Knox's men. Others went to the hostages.

No, the former hostages. They were free. They were all on their feet, laughing, crying, hugging. Everyone was safe. That fact penetrated her horror, yet her nerves had been strung too tightly for her to feel anything as simple as relief.

Help had come after all. The evidence was right before her eyes. Somehow, Mitch's message had worked.

He placed the weapons he held on the floor and led her away while agents bent over Knox's body. He didn't stop until they reached the front windows. "Breathe," he ordered. "Slow and steady. You're okay. It's over."

Chantal dropped her forehead to his shoulder. He was a rock. How many times had she turned to him, held him, shared his strength?

But the time for that had ended. They were safe. It was over, just as he'd said, as she'd wanted, as she'd prayed.

"You did great." He stroked her hair, then her back, his touch calm, as if they had all the time in the world.

But they didn't. She forced herself to straighten. "Mitch! We have to stop the shipment of missiles!"

He nodded his chin toward the other end of the lobby. "I'd guess that's tops on Graham's agenda."

She followed his gaze. Jim Whitby was being led away in handcuffs while Graham spoke heatedly with two FBI agents. They turned with him and hurried toward the back of the building, in all probability heading for the computer and the radio in her office.

A woman in a tweed suit separated from the knot of agents who were dealing with the freed hostages. She approached Chantal and Mitch. Before she could reach them, she was overtaken and passed by a tall, lanky man in a set of army fatigues.

Mitch tensed. "What the hell's he doing here?"

The soldier was carrying what appeared to be a red tackle box that had a cross made of white tape on the side. He jogged directly to Mitch and gave him a crisp salute. "Major Redinger, you'd better let me take a look at that arm."

His arm? Chantal focused on his sleeve. It gaped apart.

She remembered the leather had been sliced during his scuffle with Knox's man.

He shucked his jacket and pushed up his sweatshirt sleeve to regard his forearm. Both she and the soldier relaxed when they saw there wasn't even a scratch on Mitch's skin. "How did you get here, Norton?" he asked.

"We hitched a ride with the FBI. Officially, we tagged along as advisers."

"We?"

The soldier grinned. "The whole team's here, sir. You've pulled our butts out of the fire often enough. None of us would miss the chance to return the favor."

An answering smile deepened the lines beside Mitch's mouth. "You almost did miss it, Sergeant."

"We would have dropped in earlier if it wasn't for those pesky rules about not deploying on American soil. None of us know how to get around red tape as well as you do, Major."

"A fact the army should be grateful for. Chantal, this is Sergeant Norton, Eagle Squadron's medic. Sergeant, this is Miss Leduc, the owner of the Aerie."

"Pleased to meet you, ma'am," Norton said. He paused to look more closely at her face. "Whoa. Is any of that blood yours?"

"No. It's..." She swallowed hard and glanced back toward the spot where Knox had fallen. The remains were being loaded into a black body bag.

"Knox was leaning in front of her," Mitch said. "She caught the spray."

Norton took a plastic box of diaper wipes from what she now realized was his med kit and handed them to her. "Here. I've found these are good for cleaning all kinds of things besides babies."

He spoke as calmly as Mitch. She didn't want to think about how many times they might have needed to wipe off blood. She nodded her thanks and took one of the moistened cloths. "Major Redinger hurt his ankle," she said. "You'll need to get him to a hospital to have it X-rayed."

"Evac's standing by, Miss Leduc. We'll start moving people out as soon as the area's secured."

"We've got a prisoner locked up in one of the old cabins near the base of the hill," Mitch said.

"Duncan already got Captain Fox to point the sats this way. She's using infrared to help track down the stragglers. She'll spot him and guide the feds."

"As I recall, Norton, most of you were on leave this week."

"That's why we were late getting your message. We weren't there when Deputy Hennessey called Fort Bragg to check out your credentials. We mobilized as soon as we heard."

"What about Deputy Hennessey?" Chantal asked quickly. "And his wife? We saw Knox's men destroy their plane. Is there any chance they survived?"

Norton shook his head. "Sorry, no. Were they friends of yours?"

She nodded. In spite of how horrible Knox's death had been, she couldn't be sorry he had died. "And Waterfalls Resort? It's at the north end of the lake. It looked from here as if..."

"We're sorry, Miss Leduc." A woman spoke from behind her shoulder. When Chantal turned, the woman held out her hand. "Special Agent Sandra Templar," she said. It was the agent in the tweed suit. "The resort was leveled. I'm afraid your neighbor didn't make it, but without your efforts, many more lives would have been lost. We owe both you and Major Redinger our sincere thanks."

"Agent Templar," Mitch said. "It's good to see you again, but isn't Maine out of your area? I thought you were based in Denver."

The woman smiled. "It's good to see you too, Major. When I heard it was you calling for help, I found a way to tag along." She returned her gaze to Chantal. "Major Redinger and his team helped us out on a case a few years ago. You were fortunate he was here."

Yes, she was. Everyone was. Yet only four days ago she'd wished he'd been anywhere else. She took a fresh diaper wipe from the box. She was reaching to clean the blood she'd smeared on Mitch's neck when she was separated from him by the impact of a small body.

"Miss Leduc!" Henry wrapped his skinny arms around her waist. He laughed as he clung to her. "I *knew* you'd come back. I told them!"

"Chantal, I'm so glad you're all right." Tyra engulfed her in a hug that included her son. "It's been a nightmare. I still can't believe what happened."

Walter reached her next. His forehead bore a crusted gash and a large bruise from where he'd been struck during the initial assault, but his smile was beaming. Within moments, Rhonda and Tommy took their turns hugging her. Even the rest of Graham's staff joined the group to embrace her. Everyone talked at once, yet there was a brittle edge to their excitement.

Chantal felt sick at the thought of what they had endured. They needed food and rest more than she did. She turned to Agent Templar, demanding to know what would be done for her people. She was quickly assured the mental and physical health of the former hostages would be their top priority. It wasn't enough. Chantal still felt responsible for their welfare.

She glanced at Mitch. The army men who had been Graham's guests congratulated him with handshakes and hearty slaps on the back. Three more soldiers in fatigues like Norton had joined the group around Mitch. Judging by their size and their muscular builds, they had to be more commandos from Eagle Squadron. Though they kept their distance from him, their body language was unmistakably protective. It was obvious to her they were as concerned about their commander as the medic was.

The circle of her friends pulled her farther away as the soldiers around Mitch did the same. The distance between them grew. So did the lump in Chantal's throat.

It truly was over. Once more, she would return to her world just as Mitch would be drawn back to his.

She'd known this would happen. It had been inevitable from the start. As if he could feel her gaze, Mitch looked her way. Somehow, she dredged up her hostess's smile, or as close to one as she could manage. Turning away, she tried to regard the scene from a professional perspective.

The place was a mess. There were ragged bullet holes in the floor. Who knew what shape the kitchen and the guest rooms were in? Her watercraft were ruined. Everything in the drive shed had likely been burned to cinders. She would need to refund Graham's deposit. See? She had more than enough to fill her time and occupy her mind. Just sorting through the insurance issues alone would keep her too busy to dwell on any emptiness she might feel.

"Chantal?" Mitch touched her arm.

She jumped.

Damn, would that pattern never change?

"Chantal, we need to talk."

"Yes, I should thank you," she said. "I don't think I have yet. You handled this crisis better than anyone could have expected."

"Don't do that."

"What? Don't thank you? Don't be modest. We owe you more than words can express." She blinked hard, struggling for control. She looked around. Her staff were watching her, just as the soldiers were observing Mitch. She tried for a smile again. "Any time you want a holiday, you're welcome to come back and stay, compliments of the Aerie, of course. It's the least we can do for you to show our appreciation. Hopefully, we'll have the damage repaired by the time we open for the season next spring, although I'm not sure whether we'll be able to replace the mahogany launch."

He clenched his jaw, then put his hand on the small of her back and turned her away from the onlookers. He didn't stop until they had crossed the lobby and he had led her outside to the deck.

The stench of smoke and burnt rubber wafted on the breeze, along with the sound of voices on the hill and approaching helicopters. Her home was still being invaded, although this time by law enforcement personnel instead of thugs. For the moment, at least, she and Mitch were alone.

"Don't treat me like a stranger," he said. "It won't work."

She stepped away from him and walked to the railing at the side of the deck that overlooked the lake. The air that came over the water was fresher. It helped steady her. "Is that why you brought me out here? To complain about my manners?"

"We never finished our conversation in the cabin. Now's as good a time as any."

"I think we already said everything there was to say. Probably more than we should have. We worked well together, but the situation is over and we have to go back to real life."

He moved beside her. "Is that what you truly want, Chantal?"

No, I want you to love me.

He inhaled sharply. For a second she thought she might have said it aloud, but her lips were still pressed tightly together. No, she didn't want his love. She knew better than that. Love meant pain. Love left you weak and powerless. "I want to part as friends."

"Friends," he repeated.

"Yes. Considering our history, don't you think that's quite an accomplishment?"

"Define friends."

"Someone you know well. Someone you care what happens to."

"Like a friend who only comes to visit for a while and then leaves?"

"Three days, no matter how intense they've been, can't wipe away the effects of a lifetime, Mitch. A friend would understand that."

"We make a good team, Chantal."

"You have a team. They're waiting for you inside."

He fisted his hands on the railing. "As good as they are, even they have never managed to enter an enemy's stronghold and defeat a force of armed men with nothing more than matches, some confiscated weapons and a roll of duct tape. If we can do that, we can do anything, even work through the past."

"I told you, it's not the past that's the problem. It's who we are now."

"Then let's take more time to learn who we are now.

You said three days weren't enough. I agree. Come back to Fort Bragg with me."

"No. My life is here."

"You'll be closing up the Aerie for the winter."

"It will take me months to see to the repairs."

"I'm not asking for a commitment. I know we have obstacles between us. All I'm asking for is a chance to see where these feelings between us lead."

Something stirred in a locked corner of her heart. It was quickly smothered by a reflexive wave of panic. "I'm sorry, Mitch. I can't change who I am any more than you could change who you are. We're just not compatible."

His voice dropped. "It felt to me as if we were more than compatible, Chantal."

"I won't deny we have a physical attraction, and the circumstances we've been through led us to share more intimacy than we would have otherwise, but that's over."

"You know it was more than sex. We did make love. You can deny the word all you want, but it's there."

"On second thought, don't visit here again. It would be best for both of us if we make a clean break."

"A clean break. Like the last time."

"Yes. Exactly. Like the last time."

He raked his hands through his hair and turned to face her. "Well, I guess we're even."

The anger in his eyes made her take an involuntary step back. "What?"

"We've come full circle. We played out this scene before, only this time you're the voice of reason and I'm the one trying to hang on to a fantasy."

"Mitch—"

"How's this for more irony? If I'd taken what you'd offered all those years ago, I might have found out how wrong I'd been about you. I would have learned what a strong, resourceful and loyal woman you were, in spite of your age. You might have learned that love is nothing to be afraid of. We could have undone the damage that twisted relationship with your mother did and your scars would have healed. Hell, we wouldn't even be having this conversation because we could still be together."

Her lips parted but there was nothing she could say. The child inside her was silent, too.

Mitch was right. They'd come full circle. She recognized the pain beneath his anger, because that was how she had felt when he had rejected her.

Yet he *had* made the logical choice, just as she was doing now. It would be the best for both of them.

Then why didn't it feel right? Why did she want to walk back into his arms and stay, not for another minute or another day but forever? Why was the panic in her gut getting worse instead of better?

"Major Redinger!"

She jerked at the interruption. Mitch swore under his breath and glanced over his shoulder. "Not now, Matheson."

A blond man was running down the path beside the Aerie. He was larger than the soldiers she'd seen inside. He didn't appear to be dissuaded by the ice in Mitch's tone. He took the few steps to the deck in one bound. "Major, we need to evacuate."

"What are you talking about, Sergeant?"

"Knox has the whole place wired. There are bricks of C4 under the main joists. The timers I saw are set to blow in two minutes."

Chapter 14

Chantal's brain couldn't process the warning immediately. The words were lost in the emotions already whirling through her mind. It was Mitch's reaction that penetrated her daze. He anchored his fingers on her arm and dragged her off the deck. "Get everyone out!" he ordered the soldier. "Follow the path to the top of the hill. The trees and rock should shield us."

"I'm on it, sir," he said, racing into the lobby.

Through the side window, Chantal could see the word had already begun to spread. FBI agents cleared the room. People streamed to the exits. Many jumped from the back of the deck and ran past her and Mitch.

Chantal dug her heels into the gravel when they reached the path. "No! He's wrong! This has to be a mistake."

"Sergeant Matheson's our ordnance man. He's never wrong."

She struggled against Mitch's hold. "I have to see! Let me go!"

"Stop fighting, we have to get clear."

"This doesn't make sense. Why would Knox—"

"Plant bombs? To cover his retreat. He probably planned this from the start."

No. Please, no. It was supposed to be over. "Two minutes," she gasped. "Your man said there were two minutes."

"More like half a minute now."

"Then tell him to pull the plugs or cut the wires. Anything!"

He clamped his arm around her waist, lifted her from her feet and carried her against his hip. His limp became a lurch, but his progress up the hill didn't slow. "I won't order one of my men to throw away his life for a building."

She felt something hard press into her ribs. It was the knife she'd picked up from Knox's man. She'd put it in her jacket pocket. She wrapped her arms around the trunk of a pine tree that Mitch was passing and yanked herself out of his grip.

"Chantal!"

She ran down the path, fumbling in her pocket for the knife. If she'd been thinking straight, she would have realized she knew nothing about deactivating timers or defusing bombs, but she was operating on pure emotion. She'd just let Mitch go. She'd cut off any hope of a relationship between them. She couldn't lose this place, too. Not without a fight.

There was no one else coming from the lodge now. The path was empty. The doors had been left open. Light spilled to the ground, warm and inviting. The windows glowed in welcome, as they had on countless nights before. From the distance, over the noise of the hovering helicopters and the confused shouts of the people who had reached the hilltop behind her, a loon cried into the darkness.

The familiar sound made her steps falter. It would be all right. Sergeant Matheson must have been wrong. Mitch was overreacting. How could anyone, even a monster like Knox, want to destroy something as special as this? The Aerie would endure. It had to. It was her sanctuary.

A solid weight hit the backs of her legs. The knife flew from her grasp. Gravel stung her knees and palms as she fell to the ground.

Mitch crawled up her body. "What the hell are you trying to do?"

She twisted beneath him and pushed at his chest. "I want to save it."

"You can't." He caught her hands. "It's not worth your life."

"It *is* my life. It's all I have left."

"We're out of time. Hang on!" He wrapped one arm behind her back, hooked a leg around both of hers and rolled them off the path and toward the trees. He brought them to a stop at the base of a big spruce, cupped the back of her head and pressed her face to his shoulder.

She couldn't move. Mitch's weight pinned her down. She couldn't see. His shoulder blocked her vision. But nothing could shield her from the vibration that traveled through the ground. The blast that followed ripped the limbs from the trees around them. It sucked the air from her lungs. She had no breath left to scream.

One after another, the charges went off, turning logs into splinters and glass into a deadly rain of slivers. Mitch gathered her closer, coiling his arms around her head as debris struck the ground around them. The screech of tearing metal mixed with the roar of crumbling concrete. The noise built and deepened until it seemed as if the Aerie itself was crying.

The building was pulling away from its foundation. Timber cracked. Rock split. What remained rumbled down the hillside and crashed into the water below. Echoes bounced from the lake, replaying the destruction until they too were absorbed by the water and the night was still once again.

How many times had she thought things couldn't get worse? The worst had just happened. Chantal sobbed. It turned into a cough as she choked on the dust that clouded the air. She wrenched her arms free to push against Mitch's shoulders.

He didn't budge. Warm liquid seeped over her left wrist. For the second time in what seemed like minutes, she was feeling someone else's blood on her skin.

No. *No!*

She turned her head. Her lips brushed the edge of his jaw. "Mitch?"

He didn't respond. He still wasn't moving.

"Mitch!" she cried. She moved her hands to his back. Her right palm struck the edge of something hard. What felt like a piece of wood jutted from his back just below his shoulder. He wasn't wearing his leather jacket. He'd left it inside. There had been nothing but the fleece of his sweatshirt to protect him from the debris.

She'd been wrong. Losing the Aerie wasn't the worst thing that could happen.

Oh, God! Would this nightmare never end? She clawed at the ground behind her until she had dragged herself from beneath Mitch's inert weight. She filled her lungs and began to scream for help. Between breaths, she pulled off her jacket and pressed the sleeves around his wound to stem the bleeding.

It seemed to take forever. Her throat became hoarse from shouting, but at last a flashlight beam stabbed through the dust cloud, wobbling down the path from the hilltop.

"Over here!" she yelled.

The large blond man, Sergeant Matheson, was the first to reach them. He took in the situation at once. "It's the major," he called. "Jack, bring your kit!"

Within seconds they were surrounded by the other four commandos. Sergeant Norton knelt beside Mitch while Matheson shone the flashlight on his back.

Chantal swayed when she got a good look at the ragged piece of wood that was imbedded below his shoulder. It must have come from one of the trees. Bark was still attached to one side.

"He'll need a stretcher," Norton said. "Dunk? Kurt?"

Before he'd finished speaking, two of the men had turned and were already sprinting through the debris on their way back up the hill.

"Miss Leduc, you have to let go," Norton said. "I need to pack around that toothpick before we can move him."

"Will he be all right?"

"Sure, ma'am. It's only a flesh wound."

"Don't try that soldier-speak on me. I'm a general's daughter. I want to know how he is."

Norton motioned to her hands. She pulled them back. "It doesn't appear as if the wood hit anything vital," he said, working as he talked. "Doesn't look as if he lost enough blood to knock him out, either. My guess is some other chunk of the tree hit his head on the way down."

She skimmed her fingers over Mitch's head. "There's a lump here. Near the left side."

"Okay, it's a safe bet he's got a concussion."

"How serious do you think it is?"

"No way to tell for sure without tests, but my money's on the major. He's got a hell of a hard head."

"That's for sure," Matheson said. He squatted on the other side of Mitch. "He's one tough old man."

Their voices held both tenderness and pride. Chantal stroked a lock of hair from Mitch's forehead. "Then he should wake up soon."

"Redinger wouldn't let anything keep him down for long." A dark-haired Hispanic man knelt at her side. "He's probably thinking up a new training op while he's taking this little nap."

"Hell, yeah. He'll be pissed I didn't spot those charges sooner."

"He'll have you practicing demo with your toes next week, Junior."

Matheson frowned. "I thought for sure he'd gotten clear of the blast. His ankle must have been worse than he let on."

The man beside her grunted. "I would have carried him myself if I'd known."

"Yeah right, Gonzo." Norton took a compact, plastic pouch from his med kit and bared Mitch's arm to start an IV drip. "Ten to one he wouldn't have let you."

Chantal trailed her fingertips over Mitch's cheek. Her hand trembled. "He's the strongest man I know," she said. "He won't give up."

"He hasn't given up on any of us," Norton said. "And we're the sorriest bunch you're liable to see. The man's a glutton for punishment."

"It was my fault he got hurt. He was protecting me. He didn't think about himself. He never does. He only wants to do what's right—" Her voice broke.

The three men exchanged glances. She licked a tear from the corner of her mouth. No one spoke again until the other soldiers returned with a stretcher. "Gonzo, we could use more space."

The dark-haired soldier gripped her beneath her arms and lifted her away from Mitch. "We'll take it from here, ma'am."

"Let me help. Please."

"We've got it covered. Ready? On three."

The members of Eagle Squadron moved as one, closing ranks around their commander as they carried him up the hill.

Chantal scrambled to follow. She had to wipe her eyes to see where she was going, and the scene she'd just witnessed hadn't helped stem the tears. She'd been dead wrong to say that Mitch had chosen to live his life alone. His men were as loyal to him as he was to them. No amount of army protocol could squelch the genuine emotion they'd revealed.

Don't mistake control for a lack of feeling.

That's what Mitch had told her. And she wouldn't. Not ever again.

A helicopter with FBI markings sat on the cleared hilltop beside the black Huey that had belonged to Knox. People had gathered in clumps on the rock. No one appeared to be injured. The debris hadn't reached this far. Tyra ran toward her. "Oh, Chantal, I'm so sorry."

She tried to keep walking. "I don't think it's as bad as it looks."

"It's okay. You don't have to be brave with me." Tyra stepped in front of her, forcing her to stop. She gave her a firm hug. "You must be devastated."

"He's strong. He'll be all right."

"It hasn't sunk in yet, has it?" she asked softly, pulling back to take her by the arms. "I can understand that."

The men were heading for the FBI helicopter. Chantal looked past Tyra to keep them in sight. "Please, I have to go."

"Agent Templar says we can delay the questioning for a few days. We all need time to get back on our feet, and you need time to mourn."

"Mourn?" she asked. "Mitch isn't *dead.* He's already getting help. He'll recover. I know he will."

"Mitch? Honey, I'm not talking about Major Redinger, I'm talking about the Aerie."

The tears flowed faster. She wiped them impatiently and looked over her shoulder. The full scope of the destruction wasn't visible from here. The darkness and what was left of the trees concealed it.

"I know how you loved the place."

Yes, she had loved it. It had filled an emptiness inside her, a void that her fear had kept her from filling any other way. She had loved the walls with their smell of wood smoke and the soaring sky that had stretched beyond the windows. It had kept her safe while her heart had undertaken the long, slow process of growing up.

Growing up? Maybe it was more like *waking* up. From the whirl of thoughts and emotions that crowded her head, one thing was perfectly clear. Her love of a place could never compare to the love she felt for one proud, stubborn, flesh-and-blood man.

Yes, love. The realization hadn't come in a blinding flash. It had been working its way into her consciousness for days. Of course, she loved Mitch. He'd seen right through her attempts to deny it. Those feelings she'd had for him had never gone away. They'd just been waiting for the right time to bloom again.

That didn't mean the prospect of love was any less frightening. It was true, the habits of a lifetime couldn't be changed in three days. Mitch had been hurt by love, too. She could only hope when he woke up he would still be willing to give their relationship a chance.

"You should come and stay with us when we get back to Bethel Corners," Tyra said. "Don't go home to an empty apartment. You need time for the shock to wear off."

Chantal kissed her cheek. "Thank you for caring, Tyra. You're a good friend to worry about me after what you and your family have been through."

"That's why I'm worried. I have my family. We don't want you to go through this alone."

"I don't intend to," she said. She kissed her again and pulled out of her embrace. The helicopter's main rotor was already beginning to whirl. She ran for the door before they could close it. Mitch had said she was brave. It was time to prove him right.

She could live without the Aerie, but she couldn't conceive of a life without Mitch.

The intensive care ward of Bethel Corners Memorial Hospital was quiet this afternoon. Chantal hurried down the corridor, but she could see no sign of the men she'd shared a vigil with the night before. Eagle Squadron was gone.

Chantal wasn't alarmed by their absence. Not yet. When she'd called earlier, the doctor had told her Mitch had been awake and fully alert, so the men were probably in his room. Or they could be in the cafeteria, getting lunch. She would prefer it if they were. As much as she understood and admired their protectiveness, she was impatient for the chance to talk to Mitch alone.

He had briefly regained consciousness just before

dawn, then had lapsed into a normal sleep. It was what he needed. According to the doctor, he would make a full recovery from both the concussion and the wound in his back. His ankle might take a while longer, though. It had been more serious than a sprain—there had been a hairline fracture in one of the bones.

Naturally, he hadn't complained. He wouldn't have let on how much pain he'd been in. No, not tough-as-nails Mitch. His men were just as bad. When she'd left for her apartment, they'd been swapping stories about injuries they'd seen that had made the chunk of wood that had been in Mitch's back sound like a toothpick.

She pressed her hand over her stomach. She felt the familiar butterflies at the prospect of seeing him again. That would likely never change.

"Miss Leduc?"

She turned, smiling at the woman in the white lab coat who was walking toward her. "Dr. Gazley. I'm here to see—"

"Yes, I'm sorry. I tried calling you back. I was hoping to catch you before you left. I could have saved you the trip."

"I don't understand. You said Major Redinger was awake." She stepped toward her quickly. "Has he had a relapse?"

"Oh, no. Quite the contrary. He's already gone."

"What?"

"It was against medical advice. He should have had at least two more days of bed rest."

"He...left?"

"They all did. I can't say I'm sorry to see those soldiers go, though. They were a distraction." She winked. "Maybe now the nurses will stop finding excuses to be in ICU."

Chantal grabbed the doctor's arm. "Where did he go?"

"Miss Leduc—"

"Please, I have to know. Was it Fort Bragg?"

"I think I heard someone mention that name."

"Damn them!" she said, turning on her heel. "They knew I wanted to talk to him."

It had been almost seventeen years since Chantal had set foot on a military base. When she'd eloped with Daryl, she'd promised herself that she'd never return to one. She didn't give a second thought to the prospect of doing so now. Whatever it took, she would find Mitch.

The taxi that had brought her to the hospital was just pulling out when she reached the front entrance. She ran after it to flag it down, then chafed at the driver's sedate pace. If she'd still had her pickup truck, she could have covered the distance to her apartment in half the time.

She slammed her front door and wrenched open the closet beside it. She had just dragged out her suitcase when the back of her neck tingled. Somehow, she knew she wasn't alone.

"Going somewhere, Chantal?"

She pivoted. "Mitch!"

He was standing beside her living room window. There was a metal brace on his left foot and a white sling around his left arm. Someone must have loaned him clean clothes—his blood-soaked Patriots shirt and cargo pants had been replaced by a set of fatigues. Someone must have loaned him a razor, too. His cheeks gleamed from a fresh shave.

On some level, the details of his appearance registered, but all she really saw was his smile. She pushed aside her suitcase and crossed the floor. "Mitch, what are you doing here?"

"Waiting for you." He held out his right arm. "Where have you been?"

She laughed as she stepped into his lopsided embrace. "Trying to find you."

"We must have just missed each other."

She rubbed her nose against the hollow at the base of his neck. He'd evidently taken the time to shower, too, as she had. Yet beneath the scent of soap, he still smelled like Mitch. "That's my fault. I knew I should have stayed at the hospital, but I'd wanted the chance to clean up before you saw me again."

"Me too."

"You didn't have to."

He kissed her ear. "Neither did you. You'll always be beautiful to me, whatever you look like."

"That doesn't make sense."

"Sure, it does."

In a way, it did. Regardless of what he looked like on the outside, it was the man on the inside whom she loved. She closed her eyes, absorbing the familiar feel of him. "How did you get in here, anyway? How did you even know where I lived?"

"Not a problem. I'm from Special Ops, remember?"

"Where are your men?"

"On their way home." He kissed her forehead. "I'm sorry about the Aerie, Chantal."

"It's okay."

"No, it's not. I know how important it was to you. I'm going to contact some friends I have in Homeland Security. They'll find a way to get you compensation. That should help you rebuild."

"Homeland Security?"

"According to Intel, they intercepted the missiles as well as Knox's customer. They owe you."

She lifted her face. "Let's discuss that later."

His eyes darkened as he looked at her mouth. Instead

of giving her the kiss she craved, though, he tugged her toward her couch and sat down. "No, we really do have to talk. There's something I need to explain, Chantal."

He sounded so serious, she felt a tickle of misgiving. "Mitch—"

"It's about this," he said, lifting his arm that was in the sling.

She curled her feet onto the couch, twisting to face him. "I'm sorry you got hurt. I know it was my fault. I went a bit crazy when I heard about the bombs. I wasn't thinking."

"My injuries are nothing. That's not what I meant." He touched his right hand to his left where it stuck out of the sling. He rubbed his index finger across his wedding band. "I'm talking about my ring."

She moistened her lips. She'd been prepared for this, she reminded herself. "I apologize about that, too, Mitch," she said. "I understand there's no timetable when it comes to grief. I had no right to mention your scars, because God knows I've got enough of them myself."

"But that's the point I want to make. This isn't a scar, Chantal." He turned the ring around on his finger a few times, then slowly worked it off. "It's a tribute."

She looked from the ring to his face. "A..."

"Tribute," he repeated. "That's the only way I know how to describe it. I loved my wife. It hurt to lose her, but I will always treasure the love we had. I'm a better man for it."

"Oh, Mitch."

"I've worn this ring to remind myself of how good love can be. I'm glad I did. It's worth holding out for the real thing."

He was talking about his love for another woman. Chantal couldn't understand why it was making her fall even more in love with him. She put her hand on his thigh. "You were lucky."

"More than I could have dreamed." He pressed the ring to his lips, then buttoned it carefully into the breast pocket of his shirt. "I'd been convinced love only happens once in a lifetime, but I was wrong. Our capacity to love doesn't die. We carry it in here," he said, tapping his fingers over his heart. "I've probably loved you in one way or another for almost half your life."

She couldn't speak. She hardly dared to breathe. This was beyond what she could have hoped for.

"Remember how I told you that I thought there was a connection between us?"

She nodded. Her lips trembled.

"I'd made myself ignore it because I hadn't allowed myself to think of you as a woman. But I never forgot you. That's the real reason I accepted Graham's invitation to the Aerie. I'd known you'd be there, and I was, ah, curious."

"Curious," she repeated.

"Naturally, I also wanted some input on that signal-dampening device his company is developing," he added quickly.

She smiled. It was incredible. It seemed as if everything he said made her love him more. "Naturally. That's the kind of man you are."

"About that, I need to tell you up front, I'm an army man, so I hope you can see past your aversion to it."

She knew this was important to him, so she took time to form her response. "I respect your job, Mitch. You're a born leader, and I can't imagine you doing anything that suits you better. I would never expect you to change. I love you exactly as you are."

"Your parents weren't a good example of what marriage with a military man involves. Your mother probably would have had the same problems whatever career your father had chosen. I hope you'll come to see that—" He stopped suddenly. "Did you just say that you love me?"

"Did you just mention marriage?"

"Yes," he said simply. "I was wrong yesterday when I said I wasn't expecting a commitment. I don't want to risk losing you, Chantal. We do make a good team, and between the two of us, I'm certain we'll find a way to merge our lives. I realize this might be too fast, but—"

"Fast?" Laughing, she shifted to her knees and cradled his face in her palms. "I love you, Mitchell Redinger. I have since the moment I first saw you."

His smile was dazzling. "That's exactly what you said before."

Yes, it was. She'd known he would remember. The last time she'd said those words, she hadn't been ready for him.

She was now.

Oh, was she ever.

She touched her thumbs to the corners of his mouth. *Mitch, for heaven's sake. Stop talking already and kiss me!*

His smile changed. In spite of his injuries, he had no trouble easing her back on the couch and stretching out on top of her.

Chantal wrapped her arms around Mitch, holding on to the young man who had always held her heart.

And welcoming the warrior who had won it all over again.

* * * * *

COMING NEXT MONTH

Available August 31, 2010

#1623 CAVANAUGH REUNION
Cavanaugh Justice
Marie Ferrarella

#1624 THE LIBRARIAN'S SECRET SCANDAL
The Coltons of Montana
Jennifer Morey

#1625 PROTECTOR'S TEMPTATION
Marilyn Pappano

#1626 MESMERIZING STRANGER
New Man in Town
Jennifer Greene

ROMANTIC SUSPENSE

SRSCNM0810

Enjoy a sneak peek at fan favorite Molly O'Keefe's Harlequin Superromance miniseries, THE NOTORIOUS O'NEILLS, *with TYLER O'NEILL'S REDEMPTION, available September 2010 only from Harlequin Superromance.*

Police chief Juliette Tremblant recognized the shape of the man strolling down the street—in as calm and leisurely fashion as if it were the middle of the day rather than midnight. She slowed her car, convinced her eyes were playing tricks on her. It had been a long time since Tyler O'Neill had been seen in this town.

As she pulled to a stop at the curb, he turned toward her, and her heart about stopped.

"What the hell are you doing here, Tyler?"

"Well, if it isn't Juliette Tremblant." He made his way over to her, then leaned down so he could look her in the eye. He was close enough to touch.

Juliette was not, repeat, *not* going to touch Tyler O'Neill. Not with her fingers. Not with a ten-foot pole. There would be no touching. Which was too bad, since it was the only way she was ever going to convince herself the man standing in front of her—as rumpled and heart-stoppingly handsome now as he'd been at sixteen—was real.

And not a figment of all her furious revenge dreams.

"What are you doing back in Bonne Terre?" she asked.

"The manor is sitting empty," Tyler said and shrugged, as though his arriving out of the blue after ten years was casual. "Seems like someone should be watching over the family home."

"You?" She laughed at the very notion of him being here for any unselfish reason. "Please."

HSREXP0910

He stared at her for a second, then smiled. Her heart fluttered against her chest—a small mechanical bird powered by that smile.

"You're right." But that cryptic comment was all he offered.

Juliette bit her lip against the other questions.

Why did you go?

Why didn't you write? Call?

What did I do?

But what would be the point? Ten years of silence were all the answer she really needed.

She had sworn off feeling anything for this man long ago. Yet one look at him and all the old hurt and rage resurfaced as though they'd been waiting for the chance. That made her mad.

She put the car in gear, determined not to waste another minute thinking about Tyler O'Neill. "Have a good night, Tyler," she said, liking all the cool "go screw yourself" she managed to fit into those words.

It seems Juliette has an old score to settle with Tyler.
Pick up TYLER O'NEILL'S REDEMPTION
to see how he makes it up to her.
Available September 2010,
only from Harlequin Superromance.

HSREXP0910